William J. Berenger works as a lawyer in Auckland, New Zealand; plays rugby, does Crossfit and triathlons and basically just gets on with life.

13:39 of 15 min in the hurtbox: what a great life we lead.

orandum est ut sit mens sana in corpore sano.
fortem posce animum mortis terrore carentem,
qui spatium vitae extremum inter munera ponat
naturae, qui ferre queat quoscumque labores,
nesciat irasci, cupiat nihil

You should pray for a healthy mind in a healthy body.
Ask for a stout heart that has no fear of death,
and deems length of days the least of Nature's gifts
that can endure any kind of toil,
that knows neither wrath nor desire.

Juvenal

William J. Berenger

TRANSCENDENCE

AUSTIN MACAULEY PUBLISHERS™

LONDON • CAMBRIDGE • NEW YORK • SHARJAH

A CIP catalogue record for this title is available from the British Library.

ISBN 9781528919685 (Paperback)
ISBN 9781528919692 (Hardback)
ISBN 9781528962797 (ePub e-book)

www.austinmacauley.com

First Published (2020)
Austin Macauley Publishers Ltd
25 Canada Square
Canary Wharf
London
E14 5LQ

10th/27th Battalion, Royal South Australia Regiment

Pro Patria

Chapter 1
Inevitability

The wrath sing, goddess, of Peleus' son, Achilles, that destructive wrath which brought countless woes upon the Achaeans, and sent forth to Hades many valiant souls of heroes, and made them themselves spoil for dogs and every bird; thus the plan of Zeus came to fulfilment...

The Iliad

Snowy White's bewildered eyes searched Sergeant Berenger's face in vain in the evanescent starlight. His contortions subsiding, Snowy realised he would soon be dead. He attempted to grasp his sergeant's hand, but Berenger remained impassive. Snowy's dying vision was of Berenger's inscrutable face.

Snowy had been shot in the chest. Blood seeped through the serge fabric of his shirt. Snowy had scrambled up the sandy bank, swerving directly into Sgt Berenger's line of advance. Before disappearing into the arbutus, Snowy was thrown ignominiously back onto the stony shore, where he lay writhing at Berenger's feet. By the absence of barbed wire and obstacles, Berenger confirmed they had landed in the wrong place: damned Navy.

At 11:00 pm on 24 April 1915, before clambering from the *Ionian* onto the *Scourge*, Sgt Berenger ordered the 'diggers' of 13 Platoon, serving with the 10th South Australian infantry battalion, to load magazines; contrary to orders not to. No shots were to be fired prior to dawn; they had been ordered. Berenger had extracted more rounds for the men by advising the quartermaster, they had not yet received their full complement of 200-rounds each. The quartermaster grimaced as if he had paid for the rounds himself, but reluctantly acquiesced.

The quartermaster wore a large pair of trousers to fit his relatively large girth. Sergeant Berenger had contemptuously renamed him, 'fat-pants'. Subsequently, each man carried fully loaded magazines and a further complement of 200-rounds: damned Commissariat.

To conserve water in expectation of a long day, Sgt Berenger ordered the men not to drink from their water bottles until told otherwise. Consequently, at 1:00 am on 25 April, the diggers were grateful when they were each served a mug of cocoa by a *jack tar* aboard the *Scourge*. Berenger menacingly suggested that the *jack tar* supply the men with another, to which the sailor obsequiously obliged.

At 2:30 am, the men descended from the *Scourge*; about 30 soldiers, four seamen and a coxswain per pinnace, destined for the shore. The moon crept behind a cloud. The chill air magnified the slightest sound; not the least of which was the *putt-putt-putting* of the little steamers, emanating from behind the *Scourge* to spearhead the assault.

The *jack tars* connected three pinnaces by hawsers, (one-behind-the-other to each steamer), which none too successfully attempted to *putt-putt* into their correct position: 12-steamers, each towing three pinnaces, about 150-yards abreast totalling about 1800-yards, (in practice); ready to chug-off into the dark for the shore.

What Sgt Berenger had threatened to do to the diggers if they lost their rifles in the water should not be repeated here. However, he tempered his oaths; should they fall overboard, the saltwater would soften the hard biscuits they were issued as rations. This had elicited a cynical laugh in training at Lemnos.

The platoon commander, Second Lieutenant Faber had deferred to his sergeant, when Berenger requested he call 13 platoon, the 'diggers', to distinguish them from the rest of the company.

"It raises morale," Berenger had said facetiously, in training.

Originally, the diggers thought otherwise. At the end of an arduous and strength-sapping assault, 'digging-in' had not raised morale. But as the diggers became fitter and more disciplined, they began to appreciate their new appellation and they realised they had reduced their potential exposure to enemy fire by digging-in… and it raised morale.

The private soldiers tended to laugh nervously whilst the corporals expectorated a kind of cynical guffaw, as if there was a direct nexus between a soldier's cynicism and his experience. Upon this observation, amongst the battalion, the apex of active military experience, Sgt Berenger regarded as himself. Although the Company Sergeant Major was senior in rank to him; having not served in South Africa as Berenger had, he was not more experienced.

Sergeant Berenger instructed the men to wear two sandbags (as part of their issue for the landings) folded double, down the inside-front of their shirts. Second Lieutenant Faber had intentionally overlooked this unusual detail in his inspection at 8:00 pm on the *Ionian*. Berenger suspected Faber had again deferred to his logic as Faber had observed the diggers diving on barbed wire entanglements in training. Despite the chill of the evening, beads of sweat covered Faber's forehead, *pince-nez* glasses perched precariously on his nose, from which dripped a clear drop of mucus, as he whispered, "Very good, sergeant."

Three men would throw themselves on the barbed wire so the rest of the men would be able to safely clamber over them. All of Faber's diggers had prepared for this, as Berenger was uncertain, which three men would still be alive by the time they reached the wire obstacles. The task of whom, to select to sacrifice themselves on the wire, Berenger had allocated to the corporals.

Sergeant Berenger had discussed the problem of barbed wire with one of the machine-gun corporals, who said he'd spoken to a Japanese sailor over a mug of hot char, serving on the *Ibuki* on the trip out from Albany, Western Australia. The Japanese sailor said he knew a bloke, who had served in the Russo-Japanese war.

Judging from the ignorant gapped-tooth expression of the machine-gun corporal, Berenger deduced it was the Japanese sailor, who spoke English, not the machine-gun corporal, who spoke Japanese.

However, the machine-gun corporal said if he were defending the beach, he would construct the barbed-wire obstacles in such a way as to channel the assaulters around it, into the field of fire of his machine-gun. He explained matter-of-factly, that he would shoot Berenger with enfilading fire as he approached.

"At least…" he said, scratching his chin between thumb and forefinger, "… I think that's how the Japanese did it."

He gave Sgt Berenger a wink followed by a gapped-tooth smile to which, Berenger did not reply but looked at him dispassionately.

At 3:30 am the steamers, which had formed in disarray, were ordered to the shore. This was not conducted well. Having observed the waning moon this past week, Berenger predicted the coxswains, not having the advantage of moonlight, would close-up before reaching the shore. From their night-time exercises, he calculated the total breadth of the advancing flotilla would decrease from about 1,800 yards to no greater than the coxswains of the steamers could see or hear each other; in some cases probably less than 50 yards between each steamer.

Commanding this disorganised little flotilla was the responsibility of the naval officer in command of the pinnace on the extreme right. Although traditionally correct, Berenger did not think that commanding from the flank at night was a prescient idea under these circumstances. As it turned out, despite the calm sea, the commander remained unable to control his flotilla as it unsteadily manoeuvred towards the shore.

From time to time, on the breeze, an irritated Berenger caught the sound of *jack tars* cursing at each other to keep their distance and direction but as it precipitated, ultimately to no avail. The order of steamers had changed as some of them squeezed into the wrong sequence; an error unable to be rectified due to the advancing ships behind them, which would be compounded when soldiers disembarked at the beach.

The steamers and their angry cursing coxswains, observing in the breach with strict orders for silence, jostled; almost colliding into each other, to about 50 yards from the shore, where the sailors detached the hawsers; whereupon, the soldiers completed the journey by rowing the pinnaces by themselves.

Cross-tides further compounded their gradual drift away from their intended destination, whilst the precipice at the point of Ari Burnu (later known as *The Sphinx*), gradually loomed out of the darkness into view.

The whole flotilla closed-up onto this inhospitable point at least a mile removed from their intended destination. Berenger suspected at least one fool coxswain had been navigating towards the precipice at Ari Burnu rather than the low promontory nearer to Gaba Tepe.

Considering the Navy's dismal efforts to organise the approach to the landings, Berenger's respect for the *jack tars*, established whilst drinking cocoa on the *Scourge*, now ebbed to an all-time low. It was about to ebb even further. Fifty-yards from the beach, one of the steamers, towing troops from the 11th Western Australian infantry battalion let out a long and continuous trail of flame from the funnel. A Turkish flare shooting-up into the sky from the direction, whence they were to land, immediately followed.

A number of deductions rapidly flooded into Berenger's mind: the flare, which indicated the Turks' inability to communicate between their trenches and their headquarters, without alerting their approaching enemy, was inadequate; the ground at the landings would be arduous, and they were about to encounter withering Turkish fire.

The army had haphazardly organised its own maritime transport for the attack on Gallipoli; after the failure of Rear Admiral de Robeck's fleet to force the Narrows on 18 March. From the increased activity at the Piraeus, (a port with a long tradition of intrigue, surmounted only by Constantinople and Cairo), Berenger suspected it was a profiteering Greek, who had leaked information of the landings to the Turks.

Traditional enemies of the Turks, Berenger concluded the Greeks had likely devised many schemes for an attack on the Dardanelles but had hitherto with-held them from General Sir Ian Hamilton, Commander of the Mediterranean Expeditionary Force, thereby causing his general staff to devise their urgent plans afresh.

Military items from Mudros harbour originally belonging to Australians were found in the hands of the furtive Greek inhabitants of Lemnos. Since soldiers of the 10th South Australian battalion were appreciably too afraid of Berenger to steal military equipment, Berenger suspected the Greeks were the culprits. As for the official Greek undecided position upon whose side to take in the war, Berenger determined the Greeks were not to be trusted.

A crescendo of security breaches surrounding the impending attack had erupted henceforth, culminating in the newspaper announcement that the French planned to attack Kumkale in Asian Çanakkale. As the matter of security was entirely out of

Berenger's hands, he should have liked the Greek, who first divulged this information to be standing in front of him at this present moment so he could get his hands around his throat and throttle him. It came as no surprise to Berenger, that the landings at Gallipoli would be no surprise to the Turks.

***

Sergeant Berenger had more urgent matters to attend to. He relieved dead Snowy of his spare ammunition and left him eyes-open, staring lifelessly at the starry sky. Added to the whizz of Turkish rounds around him, a Maxim machine-gun situated in the hills commenced enfilading fire into the shingle and the disembarking men from the 9th Queensland infantry battalion.

Dispassionately, Berenger watched several Queenslanders scream as they were hit inside their pinnace. Several more Queenslanders, who disappeared over the side, did not reappear from the sea.

Upon realising the inevitability of an impending disaster, Berenger reflected on how severely he had punished the South Australians in training at Lemnos: for disembarking from the port and starboard, rather than the fore of their pinnaces; for scrambling ashore with weapons, which were wet, and for unforgivably, allowing sand to enter their barrels. The cynical smile belonged to Berenger.

The Company Sergeant Major arrived, completely saturated, "Where's Faber?" he panted.

"Don't know," Berenger curtly replied.

"OK, assemble your men, take off your packs and advance from here, I think we're in the wrong place."

"Sar' major," rasped Berenger.

When the British Guards say neither 'yes' nor 'no', but 'Sar' major', they mean, 'yes'. When Berenger said, 'Sar' major', it could have meant either, 'yes' or 'no' and in this particular instance, it meant, 'no'.

The beach was an imbroglio. Berenger moved what men he found; several hundred yards back towards his intended destination point, picking-up saturated Queenslanders as he went. About 500 yards down the beach he reached the beginning of the low promontory. Berenger bumped into Faber, who had momentarily become separated from his sergeant. Second Lieutenant Faber looked relieved to see him. He had taken the sandbag out of his shirt and wrapped it around his hand, through which, he had been shot.

Sergeant Berenger looked at his pocket-watch, (given to him by his father, Wilhelm Berenger, barrister). As the second-hand ticked through 5:00 am, he saw the dim morning sky light up in the distance. The British had begun to bombard Cape Hellas. Shortly thereafter, Berenger heard the comforting rumble of the ships' heavy guns as their shells pounded the foot of the peninsula.

"Sergeant Berenger," said Faber calmly, "We are to advance along this ridge-line until we reach the redoubt." He pointed to a steep ridge that snaked-off into the distance.

Sergeant Berenger invited Faber to advance with the first section. He distributed Snowy's 200-rounds amongst the shivering Queenslanders.

As they crept up the steep ridge, they could hear soldiers cursing and rushing in all directions through the scrubby bush. Berenger's greatest concern was that his men should be shot by one of them. They progressed to the top of the ridge. He looked back to the beach from whence they landed. The imbroglio had deteriorated into pandemonium. However, 'rosy-fingered dawn' allowed Berenger to appreciate the lovely morning. He inhaled the wonderful fragrant aroma of the arbutus on the cool breeze.

Disturbing his momentary quietude, Berenger observed labouring knee-deep through the surf toward the shore, some 1000 yards hence, the fattest pair of pants in the battalion. He was carrying something, which Berenger had never seen him carry during training exercises – a rifle. 'Fat-pants' waddled ashore and slumped in a dishevelled heap at the sandbank meeting the shingle and commenced to do what he was best at – nothing.

Second Lieutenant Faber and his men scouted-on ahead. The Turkish machine-gun had either run out of ammunition or moved. When Faber returned, he said he had found where the machine-gun had been emplaced, but it was gone. He also said that he had had a clear view of the redoubt slightly further up the ridge.

Sergeant Berenger calculated the Turks had dismantled their machine-gun and were moving to a new position – the redoubt; and that it would be in our best interests to arrive there before the Turks. Faber rallied the men and they crept into position to assault the redoubt from the flank.

Hearing the shouts and oaths of small groups of soldiers fighting with the Turks, Faber instructed his men to remain quiet and unseen whilst approaching the redoubt. They left in silence, creeping-up on hands and knees and finally on their bellies. Faber slithered the last few yards by himself. Surreptitiously peering through a gap in the sandbags, he found the redoubt had been abandoned.

After beckoning to the remainder of his troops to advance, Faber set about occupying their objective. He said he would take his men further in the direction of a Turkish track and clear the area to the front before calling his men to the new position. Sergeant Berenger was to consolidate the remaining troops at the redoubt and fire upon the Turks in order to protect the Queenslanders struggling through the arbutus further back down the ridgeline. Faber said he would be about an hour. Berenger looked at his pocket-watch. It was 8:15 am.

Sergeant Berenger could see the landing beach south of *The Sphinx* where the 9th and the 10th infantry battalions had landed. Some of the 11th Western Australian battalion and the 3rd Field Ambulance may have landed on the far side of Ari Burnu as their landing positions could not be seen from his vantage point. However, Berenger noted from the number of casualties littering the beach, many of them from the 10th South Australian battalion, laid in orderly rows near the sandbank on the shingle, that the 3rd Field Ambulance medics had picked their way back around the point.

The sight of so many South Australian casualties triggered the memory of a rumour, circulating at Lemnos, to re-enter Berenger's mind, which he had previously dismissed. He had heard 1st Australian Divisional commander Major-General Bridges had been persuaded to send Colonel Sinclair-McLagan's composite 3rd Australian infantry brigade to open the assault rather than Colonel MacLaurin's highly favoured 1st Australian infantry brigade.

The argument of the persuader as rumoured was that as casualties in the initial landings were expected to be as high as 30-percent, it might be expedient to send the least favoured 3rd Australian infantry brigade to open the assault. The persuader reported to General Bridges that he had heard most of the 9th Queensland battalion and 11th Western Australian battalion were rough, ill-disciplined miscreants; moreover most of the 10th South Australian battalion were descendants of the enemy, the Germans, and as for the composite 12th Tasmanian battalion – well.

A high casualty rate from the less prepared Australian 3rd infantry brigade would cause less ripples in New South Wales, than a high casualty rate from the sons of the well-to-do 1st Australian infantry brigade, who had all volunteered from Sydney.

General Bridges was gently reminded that the 3rd Brigade had been stationed at Lemnos since 4 March, whilst the 1st and 2nd Brigades were training in Egypt. Therefore, the 3rd Brigade was more proximate to the peninsula. A further unnecessary reminder that the Brigades were presently rated 1–3 in order of their effectiveness rather than the dates of their formation was met with a frown.

The argument that the 3rd had been stationed on Lemnos to protect the rear whilst the 1st and 2nd trained; and would protect the rear from the opposite side if the 1st and 2nd conducted their assault two-abreast, thereby becoming their strategic reserve was conveniently overlooked.

The persuader persisted. Shrewd enough not to include the word *expendable* in his argument to General Bridges, the persuader opined that a decision to send the 3rd Brigade to open the assault could be argued later in defence to a charge of recklessness, on grounds of 3rd Brigade proximity to Gallipoli, over the better military preparedness of the 1st and 2nd Brigades. He added, the Division had not yet effectively organised 1st and 2nd Brigade transport from Egypt; it was already late March and the landings were scheduled for April.

If the landings were unsuccessful due to insufficient *time* to prepare, rather than unsuccessful *efforts* to prepare the Division, this would be the error of Australian and New Zealand Army Corps commander Lieutenant-General Birdwood. Lieutenant-

General Birdwood would be culpable for failing to determine that his Corps was not yet ready, and lacking the courage to request from his superior, General Hamilton more time to train the Division, would it not?

Should this whole affair become, God forbid, a disaster; and an inquiry instigated to apportion blame, a successful argument in the Division's defence would protect the reputation of the whole 1st Australian Division. What the persuader intended by his poisonous argument was: protecting the Division's reputation would protect the persuader's reputation. What General Bridges acutely perceived was: protecting Division's reputation would protect General Bridges' reputation.

Before General Bridges curtly dismissed the persuader with a flick of his hand, the persuader suggested the 10th South Australian 'Germans', (stressing the first syllable), be positioned at the centre of the assault. Questioning these Germans' loyalty to the imperial cause should test their resolve, where the casualties are predicted to be most severe. When the casualty reports are released in the Sydney Herald or the Melbourne Advertiser, it would cause less public consternation. Berenger knew of only two persons, who had the sophistication to create and successfully propagate such a lurid and deceptive tale. One of whom, he'd served under in South Africa, and the other was him.

Chapter 2
Acceptance

"We were out on the veldt, fighting the Boer, the way he fought us. I'll tell you what rule we applied, sir. We applied Rule 303. We caught them and we shot them under Rule 303."

Breaker Morant

On 1 January 1901, William Berenger's father, Wilhelm Berenger, Barrister-at-Law, Adelaide, South Australia asked him whether he might serve in the Boer War.

"On whose side?" William tersely replied.

Without further consultation, despite William's protestations that he wanted to complete his studies in law and philosophy, William's father bellowed, "By God, you will serve your country!"

Gott ist tot, William thought to himself.

Without further ado, Wilhelm Berenger secured William's commission into the Mounted Infantry to serve with the South Australian Imperial Bushmen. There was not much William could do about the decision, but take, in retribution, Wilhelm's copy of Crime and Punishment because Wilhelm had not finished reading it. William would give it back to him when he returned and Wilhelm could suffer without it.

William's mother had died and he was an only child. At their final dinner together, William's father toasted and regaled him with tedious tales of the Franco-Prussian War. The only fact, which made the slightest impression on William, was that the Prussians had won.

William had no military experience and he ultimately expected to be in command of no one. He had spent most of the intervening time travelling to South Africa when he arrived in April 1901. His horse, procured by his father prior to sailing from Australia, had died in transit because to spite his father, rather than properly care for it, William read Dostoevsky instead. This behaviour did not bode well for a Mounted Infantryman. Upon arrival he had, like his father, not completed Crime and Punishment, but he had analysed Raskolnikov's nihilism many times.

When he first met the adjutant in Transvaal, the adjutant announced himself as de Wet. From de Wet's demeanour, William realised, like Dostoevsky's Lizaveta, he was a louse: a louse, who by rank was able to exert a pretentious kind of superiority over him. Emphasised by the way he parted his blonde hair ostentatiously down the centre in the English style, to the way he stentoriously ordered a social inferior to polish his riding boots.

William summed-up the adjutant as a fraud; and the lowest sort of advocate of Social Darwinism. By his pompous expression, de Wet revealed his jealousy to William. From William's last name, de Wet had determined from his erroneous racial theories that 'Berenger' was of German descent. According to de Wet, William was not racially superior to the English, but racially superior to the Dutch. Therefore, he genetically determined, by surname alone that William was racially superior to him. By William's mere existence, he posed a threat to de Wet and his Dutch inferiority complex.

William understood that the existence of the übermensch could not be defined in terms of racial background. William was uncertain whether the übermensch could exist at all. He concluded that the historic personage was a product of distant evolutionary anthropology, psychology and biology rather than a fashionable product of Nietzsche's imagination.

The übermensch would be found (if at all) irrespective of the confines of race or culture. On racial grounds, de Wet was wrong. William thought it sycophantic for a person of any group to cling to the shirt tails of a theory by grasping at the greatness of others, merely because of some shared racial characteristic of the group. Eventually it would be revealed to de Wet that the meaning of his pretentious existence would amount to nothing. Social Darwinists were sycophants, ipso facto, Social Darwinists were not übermenschen.

However, de Wet was a dangerous social and political survivor. He was even more dangerous to William in their present proximity. William was unable to control a wry type of scornful smile, beginning to develop on one side of his mouth, (a tendency, upon being forced to suffer a fool, which remained with him ever since), at the coincidence of de Wet's namesake, Boer General Christian de Wet. De Wet perspicaciously perceived, from William's facial expression, what he was thinking, for which, William realised he would pay. This expression would become William's Achilles' heel.

"The commandant will see you now," said de Wet ominously.

He opened the door of the commandant's office inwards, with one hand. Standing with his back to the door, he beckoned William with the palm of his other hand. The hinges of the door creaked terribly, revealing that either the commandant did not often receive guests, or it was not the commandant's office, or it was not the commandant, who would be receiving William. William held his scorn and his breath (so as not to inhale any odour from de Wet) as he squeezed past.

"Come in, come in. I'm Major Chomondley, second-in-command, acting-commandant in the commandant's absence. I'm afraid the commandant has been taken ill, but I have received your paperwork and I will advise Captain de Wet to show you to your quarters. I see you've lost your horse in transit and you speak German. That's close enough to Afrikaans, ha. We've got just the job for you. Unfortunately, I'm afraid I'm very busy at the moment. If you have any questions, be so kind as to ask Captain de Wet. I'm sure he should be more than obliged to assist."

Major Chomondley appeared by his nervous demeanour to hardly have been second-in-command of even himself. His speech was slightly slurred, his eyes were glassy and his breath reeked of spirits. Major Chomondley was the type of person, who felt uneasy about uncomfortable silences, so William said nothing, saluted, about-turned and marched out. As he approached the door, it magically opened with de Wet standing behind it.

"Come with me, Berenger."

Captain de Wet marched William from the headquarters building, which had been converted from a farmhouse in the Dutch architectural style to a kraal, where a mounted patrol had recently returned.

The horses looked underfed and the troopers appeared gaunt and tired but nevertheless they deliberately set about tending to their horses. One junior officer, the patrol leader, appeared older than de Wet by about 10 years remained motionless on his horse while his troops worked. As de Wet approached, William observed this mounted infantryman's eyes squint ever so slightly as de Wet's shadow cast long from the afternoon sun came across the hooves of his horse.

"Morant!" the adjutant's pitch was inadvertently high. This was for William's benefit, rather than for the benefit of Morant; reminding all present that Captain de Wet was the ranking officer, but by the intonation of Morant's name, revealed that de Wet was the least respected soldier of the two.

Morant continued observing his patrol attend to the details of maintaining their horses. "Lieutenant Morant!" de Wit broadcasted, accentuating an 'f' sound in the word, 'lieutenant'.

When all the troopers had completed removing their saddles and affixed nosebags to their mounts, Morant's eyes gazed down icily at a perspiring de Wet.

De Wet swallowed. William noted that Morant had observed his wry half-smile and without changing his expression, he acknowledged William's deference to him by the merest nod of his head, which de Wet did not discern.

"Morant, I want you to show Berenger to his quarters."

"Sir," Morant replied.

De Wet returned to the farmhouse and Morant, who hadn't moved an inch, continued observing his men care for their horses. When one of his troops reported to him that they were finished, Morant quietly dismissed them and began the same careful process with his own mount. When he'd finished, Morant walked up to where William was standing patiently in the burning sun. With a smile he said, "Call me, Breaker, mate," firmly shook Berenger's hand and took him to his quarters.

Quarters was a small converted barn. Austere from the outside, the interior appeared austere but gemütlich, and was a pleasant respite from the heat of the day. There were six cots: three lined-up facing the spaces between the cots against the opposite wall. The seventh cot, belonging to Breaker was concealed behind a partition made with a blanket, so he could draft his orders for the patrol, by candlelight in the evenings, without disturbing his men whilst they slept.

The cots and the equipment, which surrounded them were weathered but meticulously kept. Every item appeared to be clean, well maintained and identically arranged with every other cot except for the variety of books, which lay stacked neatly on their small bedside tables. William noted that one of the patrol had been reading Tolstoy's newly translated War and Peace and all the volumes except volume one were stacked neatly on the table against the wall. Volume one, William discovered was stacked on the table next to another cot.

"That cot's yours," said Breaker pointing to the cot nearest the door.

"Arrange your equipment in exactly same manner as you see each of the other cots and a corporal will inspect your equipment at 18:30."

Using the new 24-hour clock, as yet not adopted by the British, Breaker answered William's puzzled expression with, "6:30 pm," and disappeared behind his curtain.

"War and Peace begins at a soiree where Russian aristocrats express their fear of a French invasion," instructed Breaker, from behind the curtain.

"But the influence of Enlightenment ideas was already extant in the first chapter. The Russian aristocracy spoke French. The inevitability in War and Peace was not that the French invasion would be ultimately unsuccessful but six years before its publication; the emancipation of the serfs would cause an upheaval in Russian society. It that sense, in 1812 the Russians would be fighting a fait accompli. It is the same with the Boer. They have lost already."

Breaker paused. "Only they have not realised it yet."

Having been introduced to Breaker's patrol over supper, William was impressed by their quiet deliberateness. Introducing themselves, without frivolity, each concisely described their function in the patrol and told William their one or two syllable sobriquet, by which they preferred to be known.

Breaker spoke last.

"Berenger, we are here to fight the Boer. The Boer is not only a farmer. The Boer is also his wife, his children, his livestock, his land, his dead ancestors and his fanatic religious beliefs. The Boer is an idea. Everything animate or inanimate that comes into contact with the Boer, either eventually becomes Boer or is destroyed. If you shoot the Boer, his wife will shoot you. If you shoot his wife, his children will shoot you. If you drink out of his well, the Boer will have poisoned it previously, and you will die."

The patrol quietly finished their supper, and continued preparing their equipment for the next day's patrol. Whilst lying in his cot that evening, William worked out all the permutations of the 24-hour clock whilst watching the crescent moon through the unshuttered window. So impressed was William at the commitment of the Boer, he desired to become one himself. With that in mind, William drifted-off to sleep.

A rooster crowed outside William's window and he looked at his pocket-watch: 5:30 am. The patrol arose and prepared their breakfast. Breaker was already dressed.

"I'm not going on patrol today. Berenger, you are coming with me," he said.

William dourly watched the patrol make their way through the kraal and disappear into the veldt as he began his training with Breaker.

"I heard you let your horse die. You will not receive any training in horsemanship until I say so. You will run everywhere until I tell you to stop. Whilst doing so, you will also think about the utility of spite."

They walked to the fence enclosing the kraal. The sun had begun to rise and the moon had not yet set.

"Rule number 1: never obey an unlawful command," Breaker said.

The rules, all delivered orally, were not too difficult to remember. It was the exceptions to the rules and their practical application that required constant attention and practice.

"Our first lesson will be in navigation. I will teach you how to locate north by the sun. Look directly at the sun."

Breaker's hand clubbing William to the side of his head, reinforced rule number 1: never obey an unlawful command.

"Give me your pocket-watch."

Breaker laid the pocket-watch, flat in the palm of his hand, with the numeral XII, in line with the sun.

"Point the XII in the direction of the sun. In the Southern Hemisphere, north is approximately halfway between the XII and the hour hand."

"If I confiscate your pocket-watch, and told you at 15:00 hours, the sun will be directly above the rocks on the hill over there," he said pointing to a rocky outcrop, "Where is north?"

William laid an imaginary pocket-watch in the palm of his hand and pointed the XII in the direction of the rock. He thought for a moment, bisecting the imaginary XII and the III on the palm of his hand, and pointed to the dusty track, meandering away from the farmhouse. Breaker nodded again.

"You do not need a watch to find north by the sun. You only need to know the time."

"Night navigation: look at the moon." Berenger hesitated momentarily, and looked at the moon still in the morning sky.

Breaker half smiled.

"The moon is a crescent. Draw an imaginary line from the tip of the crescent at the top through the tip of the crescent at the bottom and extend the line to the horizon."

Berenger smiled when he completed his calculations. He confirmed north as the dusty track leading away from the farmhouse.

"You no longer need your pocket watch. I will deliver it to the farmhouse, where it will be kept with de Wet until you leave. You will train without it until I tell you otherwise. Reveille is at 5:30."

William knew the rooster would wake him up.

"The next out-post is five miles north along the track. It is another farmhouse like ours. You have two hours to tell me what colour the roof is. When you return, you will receive the receipt for your pocket-watch. Unless you have any questions…Go!"

William ran out the gate and followed the track winding upwards around undulating barren hills until after about three miles, he could make out the little farmhouse in the distance with a red roof. The chimney, despite the warm weather, produced comforting puffs of grey-white smoke.

William stopped to re-orientate himself and observe the harsh dry landscape; a dry streambed and a leafless tortured tree refusing to die. Collecting his thoughts, he turned back down the track leading to the kraal; this time counting his steps as he ran three miles home.

When William returned, Breaker was gone and he received the receipt for his pocket-watch from a one-armed Bantu servant at the farmhouse. Over the weeks that followed the servant watched William running about, in and out of the kraal. One hot afternoon, William saw the servant struggling to polish de Wet's riding boots. William thought he was flapping about so he ran up to him. The Bantu slowly stood up.

"I've been watching you," he said.

"You speak English," William said.

"Yes. I've been watching you and I think you have been working hard."

William said nothing.

"I will tell you how to predict the weather up to one week hence and the patrol will respect you."

"Why?" William's eyes narrowed.

"Because the Boer cut off my arm."

***

Training went on incessantly day and night, each senior member of the patrol taking it in turns to impart their knowledge to William on the day they were allocated to remain at the farmhouse. Although William already knew how to ride, he was as yet given no further instruction on maintaining horses but for mucking them out, which was one of his daily punishment duties.

Shooting accurately appeared to be Breaker's priority for William after about a week's induction at his camp. Breaker could shoot either mounted or dismounted. William was taught only how to fire from various dismounted positions for reasons which, Breaker did not need to explain to him. The patrol used either a Martini Henry or a Lee Enfield carbine. William practised with one of the Mausers and the Mauser ammunition that the patrol had taken in a raid of a Boer farmhouse. Weapons practise was conducted and tested almost every day.

Breaker said the round left the muzzle on a parabolic trajectory. William was to determine the maximum range of the Mauser by trial and error; determine the height of the parabola and zero the weapon without much further information than that, which Breaker had already delivered. Breaker's Socratic training methods were challenging and the three tasks took about a week and hundreds of rounds of ammunition to complete accurately.

Fortunately, William had the evenings to attempt to mentally calculate the height of the parabola in his cot as he watched the moon wax through the unshuttered window. William was disappointed to learn that he hadn't even started shooting yet when he correctly demonstrated the answers.

William was made to run everywhere, which he did religiously to avoid further punishment until he began to enjoy its redeeming benefits. One day whilst mucking out the stalls in the large barn, William noticed the horse belonging to the corporal, who had been instructed to remain behind to conduct William's training. The creature was emaciated. William looked into its big dumb face and determined that like William, he too was suffering.

William acknowledged this starving horse's stoic nobility by removing him from his stall and placing him in the stall, which best allowed the gentle breeze to cool him. William then mucked out his stall and allowed him to remain in the slightly cooler one until just before the patrol returned.

One evening after supper, Breaker announced that the patrol would be gone longer than usual. In his cot that evening, William thought about the weather conditions for the following days. William arose before the rooster crowed, took one of his white sheets and put it in the black servant's dhobi bag. He took a clean sheet from the line, which hung between the farmhouse and the small barn, from which he made six bandanas. William folded the bandanas carefully and espied a water-canteen beneath the stoep of the farmhouse. Later, William found out that it belonged to de Wet.

At breakfast, Breaker broke the execution of the patrol into the minutest details so that every member knew what he was to do in the event of any contingency. At the end of Breaker's brief, there was a discussion session after which, William produced the six bandanas and the extra water-canteen.

William said, "Three days hence there will be a dust storm. You will need these to cover your faces."

For a few seconds there was silence.

Then Breaker said, "Good on ya, mate."

The patrol looked at each other and the corporal slapped William's back. Two of the others shook his hand and William received a couple of cynical smiles and laughs, which were returned in kind. Finally, William felt accepted. Acceptance: one of the most sought after, most precarious, fleeting and elusive of human desires. In retrospect, William wondered whether his suffering in pursuit of acceptance was suffering at all. From his present perspective, it certainly seemed worthwhile to him in the long run. He started to doubt the existence of suffering as an absolute.

Breaker said William should patrol more slowly around the camp perimeter after first light from now on as he would be better able to observe any sign that the Boer had been near the camp. William felt honoured.

William had not reckoned that de Wet would invite himself on the patrol. De Wet had not even attended the briefing and he had lost his water-canteen. He was furious. De Wet was too proud to admit to the patrol he had lost it; ultimately to his own detriment several days later. De Wet had, as William was to find out later, stolen his pocket-watch.

After the patrol had set off, the camp belonged to the one-armed Bantu servant, Major Chomondley, who rarely left his little office, and William. William often heard Major Chomondley singing drunken bawdy songs to himself in his office late in the evening. On the afternoon of the day on which, the patrol was scheduled to return, William set off with his Mauser, ammunition and a few provisions for the point on the track north where he could see the little farmhouse at the next out-post in the distance.

He took a position where he was able to observe the most wonderful sunset. Shortly before last light, Berenger observed six horses in the distance.

When they were close, William whispered, "Halt."

"Breaker," said the first rider and his horse walked on through. William recognised all the voices until that last one said, "Captain de Wet," so William shot him in the chest.

Within an instant, all the riders had dismounted and taken a defensive position in the grass. Breaker slithered up to me.

William said, "I didn't recognise de Wet's voice."

28

Breaker said de Wet had suffered heat stroke and had remained at Camp K_. The voice belonged to a Boer, who had tried to slip into the rear of the patrol.

The patrol waited silently in their defensive position until first light.

When Breaker said, "They've gone. Well done, mate." The patrol returned to camp.

After tending to the animals and their kit, all the patrol were on punishment duty for failing to detect the Boer that infiltrated them whilst riding back to the farmhouse. Breaker was hardest on himself for not training the patrol properly. Actually, their training was no different than usual. Breaker only called it punishment to make them feel bad.

"Come here," Breaker said to William.

"De Wet told me to tell you that you are going to Camp K_ tomorrow morning. That is where you will remain until you to return to Australia."

Berenger did not want to leave the patrol because he wanted to model himself on Breaker Morant. William had heard about the concentration camps and thought that if he wanted to make the best of his circumstances and could not become a barrister, he would do his very best to undertake an equally respectable profession. He would become a concentration camp guard.

Chapter 3
Rejection

"She was a frail, weak little child in desperate need of good care. Yet, because her mother was one of the 'undesirables' due to the fact that her father neither surrendered nor betrayed his people, Lizzie was placed on the lowest rations and so perished with hunger…"

Emily Hobhouse

William approached Camp K_. He saw no enclosure and no guards, just off-white canvas circular tents, spaced English style, row upon row, and a few buildings to one side. But for the fact that it smelt like death, it looked quite nice and orderly. The inmates appeared to be going about the business of 'getting-by'.

Out of the corner of his eye, William saw a slim, attractive-looking woman, wearing a dark conservative full-length dress, done up at the throat with a simple white-lace trim, complete with bonnet. She was standing next to a tree stump with a small axe chained to it, blue-grey eyes blazing with hatred and fists clenched.

William looked at her impassively and made for the small farmhouse, which he had determined to be headquarters of Camp K_. Entering without knocking, he looked at the surprised face of the man seated behind his pretentious desk, incongruous with its humble surroundings.

The face contorted itself from shame to guilt, to fury; followed by a self-satisfied smile. He draped his hand with contrived nonchalance over a gaudy engraved box, informing William, by his actions that his pocket-watch was held within.

"That's Major de Wet, Berenger. I'll thank you to knock before you enter my office." Actually, William had not as yet said anything.

"Stand at attention, Berenger."

Berenger stood silently for about 30 minutes as de Wet grandiosely explained the purpose of his concentration camp, and William's function in it. On his desk sat a porcelain model of a phrenologist's head inscribed with a grid of mental faculties allocated in a pseudo-scientific manner, to which de Wet believed he possessed them all in abundance.

De Wet emphasised the gravity of allocating food correctly.

"Refugees are to be issued subsistence rations and Undesirables are to be issued half-subsistence rations. Undesirables are the wives and children of Boer commandos, who have not yet surrendered."

William determined that 'half-subsistence' was de Wet's euphemism for starvation rations. De Wet showed William a file, which was open on his desk.

"Look here, this one, Kruger, lost the youngest of her five children this morning."

Before him, William was shown, a photo of the angry woman, whom he had seen outside, below which, were names, in descending order of age, of her five children: Juliana, Geertje, Peter-Lambertus, Magdalena and Johannes. Johannes, a toddler, who had died this morning, had a neat line ruled across his name.

"Kruger's details are written here, here and here," he pointed out to William.

William noted that the questions were written in English but the answers were written in Afrikaans. "For example…," de Wet waved the file in front of William's face.

"… Full name: Cornelia Juliana Kruger; Husband: Johannes Cobus Kruger; Occupation: Helmet-Maker…."

William perused the file. The answers had been written by the inmate herself. Juliana, intentionally concealing her husband's occupation, wrote 'Hoedemaker', indicating her occupation as 'Milliner' not 'Helmet-Maker'. To William, Juliana's husband's occupation was obvious: Boer commando. In William's mind, De Wet, due to his tardiness and arrogance had yet again fallen to the bottom of the intellectual ladder.

"You speak German. I want you to interrogate her. We have not yet found her husband."

Concealing his face by turning towards his office window, De Wet stood with his hands behind his back.

"You are urgently required to become the Commander of Camp K_, Sanitation and Disposal," he said furtively.

31

Realising that de Wet spent much of his time in his office inventing absurdly bombastic titles for jobs that nobody wanted; William determined that he was in charge of the Burial Details.

Before De Wet dismissed him, William concluded that he had not seen any guards because there was an epidemic at the camp, hence the urgent requirement for a Burial Details commander. The incumbent had died of disease, to which de Wet also desired William to succumb.

When William left the farmhouse, the Boer woman, Cornelia was waiting outside.

"Sir, the children are dying," she said matter-of-factly.

Considering that de Wet desired William to join them, he decided that he had found an ally: the enemy of your enemy is your friend.

"Show me your tent."

Cornelia strode purposefully away.

"This is the residence of the Commander of the Undesirables. These are my children: Juliana, Geertje, Peter-Lambertus and Magdalena."

Four sets of gaunt eyes looked at Berenger from emaciated faces. Magdalena just lay on the ground breathing almost imperceptibly and staring straight up at the off-white canvas ceiling.

There were only two makeshift beds, two chairs and a small table near the entrance flap. Upon the table was a candle and an antique porcelain piece of blue-Delft china. William told Cornelia that they were allies. She did not believe him. William told her about de Wet, and he reluctantly disclosed some personal information as to his childhood and his home in South Australia to encourage her to forward information about her husband. All the while, Cornelia's boertjie daughter, Juliana, some 10 years William's junior, who only spoke Afrikaans, listened intently as if memorising the sounds of his words.

At the end of their discussion, Cornelia had not disclosed any information about her husband, and to prematurely engender her trust William had mistakenly disclosed details about himself. Cornelia had won this contest of wits.

In their discussion, they agreed on a number of urgent matters: unless those who were sick were separated from those who were not, they would all die from the epidemic. Those

Undesirables, who survived the epidemic, would die of starvation. They talked by candlelight long into the evening, until De Wet appeared at the flap.

"Lights out," he snapped.

William purposely ignored him and spoke to Cornelia in German; a language de Wet did not understand. William and Cornelia sat facing each other deep in conversation. De Wet was side-on to them at the entrance to the tent. The candle sat on the table next to the blue-Delft; the blue figures on the white porcelain dancing in the flickering light. De Wet became mesmerised at the figures and a look of horror over-came his face. He started shaking. Appearing to be frothing at the mouth, with the back of his hand, he knocked the blue-Delft from the table, which broke on the ground and he returned unsteadily to the farmhouse.

Cornelia raised her hands in anguish, but held her composure for fear of waking her children.

"Cornelia, do you have a picture of Jesus?" William asked calmly.

Cornelia's blue-grey eyes burned at the apparent irrelevance of William's question.

"We do not worship idols," she hissed, referring to her iconoclastic Calvinism.

"Do you have an image of Jesus in your mind when you pray to him?"

"Yes," she answered.

"Do you have an image of the blue-Delft in your mind even though the pieces of porcelain scattered on the ground no longer exist as the blue-Delft?"

Cornelia's anger dissipated as she considered William's question. No answer, but William could see Cornelia was thinking, so he continued.

"There is more to Art, then the object itself. We acknowledge the Beauty of the blue-Delft irrespective of whether the blue-Delft remains in existence, do we not? The Beauty of the blue-Delft is not extinguished when the blue-Delft no longer exists."

William paused for a few seconds.

"By ignoring de Wet, we denied his existence. So, de Wet destroyed the blue-Delft, but not the blue-Delft's Beauty. He has come to the realisation that without recognition his existence is meaningless. But we both already knew that too. I expect madness will shortly follow de Wet's descent into depravity."

Cornelia understood that the physical destruction of her simple blue-Delft did not extinguish its Beauty, but she started to cry whilst picking-up the broken pieces of porcelain, so William left.

The next morning, whilst conducting a clearing patrol with his Mauser around the perimeter of the camp, William discovered a graveyard on a small hill over-looking the veldt. The unburied corpses of an old man, a woman and her several children lay close together.

When William returned to camp, he heard a commotion coming from one of the tents. William saw de Wet dash out followed by a boer oma, who had detached the small axe and chain from the tree stump, cursing in Afrikaans and intent on smashing the axe into de Wet's head. William also noticed that de Wet had a much smaller chain dangling from an item clutched in his hand, which he recognised to be his pocket-watch.

"Berenger, shoot her!" de Wet screamed as he ran towards William.

William raised his Mauser, calmed his breath and fired. The round nicked de Wet on the wrist, causing him to drop the pocket-watch and killed the old woman pursuing him.

The cry of the old woman's granddaughter drowned de Wet's protestations, "Berenger, you've shot me, you fool."

William picked up his pocket-watch and looked at de Wet to which, he sneered, "I'll have you hung for this."

Holding his mildly injured wrist, he limped back to his office leaving the girl crying upon her oma. But for Cornelia, who went to comfort the girl, everyone else in the camp just went back to work.

In the next few days, Cornelia confided in William that the girl said de Wet had tried to bribe her oma with the pocket-watch in exchange for favours with her granddaughter. William knew that de Wet would charge him for shooting him in the wrist, so he said nothing.

William noted that the guards and commissariat wagon no longer entered Camp K_ but, at the camp entrance, distributed the weekly food rations to representatives of the Refugees and Undesirables, who subsequently redistributed it to the inmates.

Cornelia, as senior representative of the Undesirables, apportioned the meagre rations under the scrutiny of the female-head of each family.

Their equanimity would not have been lost amongst the men of the *Batavia*. However, on closely, observing Juliana further subdivide her allotted ration, William noted that she redistributed her rations disproportionately, taking some small amounts each from Magdalena, Peter-Lambertus and Geertje in order to give to Juliana. Cornelia had decided that Juliana as the eldest, was the strongest and the most likely to survive.

Although Cornelia had no power to prevent them from all dying, eventually; God's predestination had not determined, who would die last. William often saw Cornelia eat nothing and he concluded that Magdalena, Peter-Lambertus and Geertje were kept alive in order to secure their portion of rations for Juliana, who was unaware of Cornelia's scheme. Cornelia willed herself to stay alive to care for Juliana, who if the war ended after Cornelia died, would be the sole survivor of the Kruger family.

After about a week, William went to de Wet's office, bit his tongue and saying he was sick, coughed blood all over de Wet's desk with him seated behind it. De Wet went berserk. Hiding his face in his sleeve, he ran madly about the room before retreating into a tiny cramped larder, from which, he spoke to William through the door.

William said that they needed to re-organise the tents by those, who were sick and those, who had not yet caught the epidemic. William said that parts of the unburied corpses in the graveyard had been eaten by wild animals and that it was only a matter of time before the epidemic spread to the British, who came to check the camps with the weekly commissariat wagon.

Using de Wet's words against him William said that they would be able to use the inmates to properly sanitise and dispose of the dead. He had concluded that the application of Australian social justice in this war was entirely at odds with its British counter-part. However, de Wet, who had imprisoned himself in the larder, was in no position to resist. He signed the requisition form, which William had slipped under the door.

When the supplies arrived in the evening, William received them by giving the senior guard the signed requisition form. As he read it, William coughed blood on him, so he ran away. The representative from the commissariat watching William's convulsions jumped from his cart, leaving the supplies and horses, and ran after the guard back down the track.

Only William, as de Wet's prisoner and de Wet, who had locked himself in the larder, were left to guard about 100 prisoners left alive at Camp K_. William set-about rearranging the occupancy of the tents by those, who were ill and those who were not, thereby removing the distinction between Refugee and Undesirable.

Cornelia and the other women organised, who would care for the sick and how to divide the food. William had ensured that rations would be requisitioned for 200 inmates rather than 100, and de Wet had authorised and signed the requisition form.

William organised the older and healthier children of the camp into a detail, which included Juliana, to bury the dead. William made bandanas from a sheet, which they wore wrapped around their heads in such a way, as much, to conceal their tears, as the odour of death.

After about a week, they had completed burying the dead and kept up with the diminishing numbers of inmates dying from disease. William saw de Wet's mad face at the window at the back of the larder from time to time, but every time de Wet saw him, he ducked away.

The numbers in Camp K_ remained stable for a further week, William sensed the resignation of his Burial Detail to complete their daily routine as something undesirable but inevitable. He gradually allowed Juliana to take charge of digging the extra graves.

A further week passed and commissariat quickly dropped-off their supplies without allowing William to approach and then resolutely left to return to their base, whilst De Wet, remaining locked in his larder, peered from his window. Cornelia, who had volunteered to take care of the sick, became sick herself. William shaved Juliana's head, saying that it would keep the lice away, but Cornelia knew it was to make her look less desirable to the new guards, whom William predicted would arrive to take him into custody soon.

William took over delivering food to Cornelia, who in her sickness and physical weakness had aged terribly. A few of days later, when William appeared at her tent, he found her serenely dead in her cot. Magdalena and Geertje, who had died of malnutrition, snuggled up in her arms, and Peter Lambertus was sprawled dead on the dirt floor, had been apparently too weak to assist them. Juliana had already gone to work at digging graves so William gave the food to the children next door advising the eldest child, all of about eight years old to divide the rations equally amongst herself and her two younger twin brothers.

William briskly walked to the graveyard to inform 11-year-old Juliana that her family were dead and she would have to arrange their burial. When they returned to Cornelia's tent, Juliana flung herself across her mother's chest. The last William saw of Juliana was the back of her bald head, as she sobbed over her deceased mother and siblings.

William returned to the graveyard, deciding to give Juliana the afternoon off to arrange the funeral of her family. He selected a replacement Burial Details commander in her absence. In the distance, William could see a faint cloud of dust arising from the track leading to Camp K_ and realised that soon he would be taken into custody by the relieving soldiers.

He instructed the Burial Detail to stop work and stand at attention, from tallest to shortest, in a neat line on top of the hill over-looking all the graves and the veldt in the distance. William requested the replacement Burial Details commander to come out from the rank of stand next to him, which the boy did with great ceremony. William made a small speech praising each of them by name of what a wonderful job they had done keeping up with all the digging.

After William handed over command to a 10-year-old, he shook hands with him and the boy beamed with pride. They all waved goodbye to each other and wished each other well. The soldiers and the commissariat wagon had just made it to Camp K_, so William left the children happily digging their own graves and voluntarily marched into custody.

Chapter 4
Uncertainty

"It's touch and go. If the Turks come on in mass formation… I don't think anything can stop them."

Colonel Ewen Sinclair McLagan
Commander 3rd Australian Infantry Brigade

Berenger was found not guilty of intentionally shooting Captain de Wet at his trial in South Africa but he was stripped of his commission, to the disappointment of his father, who was attempting to become King's Counsel in Adelaide.

William had not returned to Australia a war hero, but as a private soldier and a disgrace. Remaining in the army in South Australia, William diligently worked through the ranks. He had been promoted to sergeant after 12 years of hard work by the outbreak of the Great War.

***

As Berenger had seen the first New Zealanders of the 3rd Auckland Infantry Regiment wading ashore at Ari Burnu, he decided Faber had taken at least an hour longer than expected. They had secured the redoubt but he was aware a concerted Turkish counter-attack could drive them back into the sea.

Sergeant Berenger discussed this with the men. Having considered their opinions, he decided that a section commander, two of his men and he would scout ahead to look for Faber. The remainder of the men would remain at the redoubt.

The four of them descended into a dry dere. Hearing the battle raging from the Queenslanders and the Turks in the valley to their left, they encountered no resistance as they advanced up another steep slope. They crept up a ridgeline to discover they were a ridge ahead of the nearest advancing troops. Berenger crawled to the summit and heard a soldier shouting orders in Turkish.

Peering through the scrub, Berenger espied a barracks below, capable of housing about 50 men, a few other buildings, a cart carrying ammunition boxes, and the detritus of soldiers, who had abandoned their position in a hurry. A Turkish voice, obscured from his view by a concrete bunker directly in front of him, barked out a name: "Ali!"

Ali appeared at the entrance at end of the barracks nearest Berenger, and ran towards the voice. After Ali, an Arab boy of about 18, had taken about three paces, a tirade of Turkish abuse came from the voice. Ali stopped, turned about, and dashed back into the barracks to retrieve his rifle.

This time when Ali appeared, the Turkish voice started barking orders at him. Before Ali had reached the concrete bunker, obscuring Berenger's view, a giant Turkish soldier marched towards a group of about eight Turkish soldiers. They appeared from a door at the far side of the barracks carrying their dissembled machine-gun and ammunition. The giant Turk started barking orders at the men, but in a less humiliating way that he had barked orders at Ali. The soldiers departed into the scrub and the giant Turk disappeared behind the barracks.

Ali was both the least liked and least proficient soldier of the group; he had been left behind for a purpose Berenger had yet to determine. Due to Ali's name, apparent Arab ethnicity, and the disparaging manner, in which the giant Turk shouted commands at him, Berenger concluded the giant Turk was a Sunni and Ali was a Shia.

In the giant Turk's racism and sectarian intolerance, Berenger determined that he had created in Ali, an eventual ally. Upon further inspection, Berenger saw a signal mirror shine through the barred ventilation window of the concrete bunker. Discovering the purpose for which Ali had been left behind, he thought to himself, *Found them.*

The Turkish soldiers left their barracks all but abandoned; and the bewildered Ali had been instructed to guard Faber and his troops, imprisoned in the concrete bunker. Berenger crept back down to the three other men and described the whereabouts of Faber and the imprisoned men. He instructed them to return to the redoubt and brief the redoubt commander; then return to his position with reinforcements, even if they had to make their way back to the beach to guide the New Zealanders to his position. As they scrambled off, they encountered rifle fire.

Cut off by Turkish rounds whizzing about him, Berenger crawled back to the top of the ridge to give the men covering fire but they had spread out; gone to ground and had commenced firing back. Shots were intermittently exchanged between both parties, crawling around in the arbutus, without apparent success from either side. Berenger determined that the Turkish soldiers had divided into two groups, leaving some riflemen to deal with the South Australians whilst the remainder proceeded with the machine-gun to a new firing position. The men were fighting their war, side-on to the Queenslanders, who would presently be advancing down the dere.

Shots were being exchanged from such concealed positions that Berenger was unable to see or detect with any certainty, who was shooting at whom. In order to better assist them, Berenger had to move. It was less than 50 yards now from the concrete bunker. Berenger intended to capture the Arab boy for interrogation and release the prisoners to reinforce the three South Australians presently fighting with the Turks.

He sprinted down to the concrete bunker, noticing two of Faber's fingers appearing high up through the barred ventilation window. As Berenger rounded the corner, he encountered Ali, who looked at him with a vacant grin. There was a searing pain in the back of Berenger's head, an explosion of stars before his eyes and then nothing.

***

"Sergeant Berenger," he heard Faber whisper.

Drifting in and out of consciousness, Berenger found he had been locked in the concrete bunker with Faber and his men. Faber's two fingers appearing at the ventilation window meant that there were two guards, not one, whose voices he could now hear arguing in Arabic, outside their little prison. As Berenger had rounded the corner of the concrete bunker, whilst confronting Ali, the second Arab had struck him in the back of the head with the butt of his rifle.

To keep him conscious, Faber started talking about his theory of quantum mechanics. He explained that particles of light had been recently named photons by the New Zealand physicist Ernest Rutherford. Photons exhibited both the characteristics of particles and the characteristics of waves, but Faber believed that at any particular moment in time, photons could only be located exhibiting the characteristics of particles.

Faber understood that sub-atomic particles, like electrons also exhibited characteristics of particles and characteristics of waves. He believed that electrons were waves, but when attempting to locate the position of an electron in an atom, at any particular moment in time, the electron, like the photon particle of light could only be located exhibiting the characteristics of particles.

"Therefore…" Faber deduced, "… electrons may exist in an atom, at more than one place at the same time. But if attempting to locate an electron in an atom at any particular moment in time, the electron may only exist in one place in the atom or not at all depending upon the moment in time when the electron is attempted to be located."

"Let me explain…" he continued, observing the shadow, which appeared on his raised hand, caused by sunlight streaming between the metal bars cemented into the bunker's window frame.

"The bars in the window form two narrow parallel spaces for sunlight to pass through. This will cause a pattern on my hand exhibiting the characteristics of waves. However, at any particular moment in time, when attempting to locate a photon of light, the photon will only exhibit the characteristics of particles. The spaces between the bars will cause some photons of light to pass through, and some photons of light will reflect off the bars."

"The pattern of light observed on my hand indicates the probability of the photon existing at any particular moment in time; where there is no light, the probability of the existence of a photon at any particular moment in time is zero. At that particular moment in time, the photon does not exist."

Berenger thought for a moment and said to Faber, "Do you believe God exists eternally?"

"Yes," Faber said.

"By eternally, do you believe that God exists and has existed, permanently?"

"Yes."

"Do you believe that God could exist in an atom?"

"Of course."

"If God existed in an atom, according to your analogy, and if we attempted to locate God in an atom, at any particular moment in time, is it possible that we may find that God may or may not exist?"

No answer.

Berenger waited a few moments.

"According to your analogy, if you believe God exists eternally, and we are unable to locate Him, in an atom, then God does not exist eternally."

Muted rifle fire could be heard in the distance as the members of the patrol locked in the concrete bunker had stopped talking at listened intently to their discourse.

Faber dropped Berenger's head onto the concrete floor and stood up. Urgent Turkish shouts resonated from without their prison, and the sound of more Turkish soldiers rushing past. Shots and a loud hail of bullets, some embedding themselves in the bunker whizzed about outside.

Sergeant Berenger heard the distinctive sound of New Zealanders angrily cursing; clipping their vowels as they pursued the Turks towards the bunker. Faber produced his signalling mirror and held it to the ventilation window only to be shot through his uninjured hand by an over-enthusiastic Auckland infantryman, named Campbell. Berenger lay on the floor breathing shallowly, listened to Campbell being referred to, as f_ Campbell by an irate superior, and drifted off into unconsciousness.

When Berenger awoke, he found he had been propped up, knees to his chest, against Faber. Joining them in their already cramped quarters were three New Zealanders from the 3rd Auckland . Infantry Regiment. The firing had stopped immediately outside but continued to rage further in the distance.

The metal door of their prison swung open, and as the setting sun's rays gushed in, the silhouette of the giant Turk appeared. He grabbed the nearest soldier by the head, dragged him out kicking, screaming and struggling and slammed the door. The soldier was kicked and beaten mercilessly whilst being dragged behind the ammunition cart round and round the concrete bunker to increase the psychological effect on the prisoners inside. The soldier's screams subsided after a solitary shot outside the prison door.

There was silence as the prisoners sat squeezed together wondering, who would be next. Berenger looked at the faces of the men in the bunker as the last rays of light from the setting sun of April 25 streamed through the ventilation window. A solemn solicitor's clerk from South Australia was sandwiched between two burly bushmen from North Queensland; a physicist from Adelaide crouched next to a farmer from South Auckland. Sticky with congealed blood dripping down his face, Berenger painfully pushed himself to his feet from Faber's shoulder. Each soldier looked at him in the eyes, in the hope that he had determined a plan of escape; some would face their executioner defiantly, some had already resigned themselves to die.

To fortify these soldiers' minds from divulging information to the enemy before their impending execution: a dramatic pause. Berenger looking at each man facing death, raised his eyes to the ceiling as if seeking inspiration and calmly said, "A Queenslander, a South Australian and a New Zealander walk into a bar…"

Chapter 5
Contrition

The Food

"...Do not be afraid of them but have fear of Me. On this day I have perfected your religion, completed My favours to you, and have chosen Islam as your religion. If anyone not inclined to sin is forced by hunger to eat unlawful substances instead of proper food, he may do so to spare his life. God is All-forgiving and All-merciful."

The Noble Qur'an (5:3)

Ali's father, Ibrahim and his family walked from Ur to Çanakkale, beginning when Ali was seven years' old. By the time Ali was 14, they had arrived. Ali was the youngest of three brothers. He had a mild learning disability. Like his family, Ali was illiterate; no matter how hard he tried, Ali could never please his father. No one ever protected Ali when he was ridiculed or beaten up. But despite Ali's baleful existence, he believed resolutely that if he accepted Allah and followed the laws of Islam, he would after death enter paradise.

Ali's learning disability increased after being beaten up so severely that he suffered further brain damage; leaving Ali with a permanent, vacant expression that would remain whilst suffering subsequent beatings, enraging the persecutor to inflict ever more serious punishment.

Ibrahim told Ali that he was named after the cousin of the prophet Muhammad, the first Shi'a imam; and this was a blessed name. But over the years, the further into Sunni territory that Ibrahim and his family migrated the more persecution was heaped upon Ali, (whose name revealed his Shia origins to the Sunni), until he felt utterly alienated and alone.

Ibrahim, a poor subsistence farmer, whose wife died giving birth to Ali, was told by his imam that life would be better if he and his family migrated west; and the further west, the family migrated, the better life would be. Simple Ibrahim believed this to be the truth because the imam had said it. The further west that Ibrahim migrated, the more disappointed life became for his family, so Ibrahim continued to migrate even further west in the hope of a better life.

Ali often ate alone, and sometimes there was not enough food for Ali to eat anything. At these times, far worse than having no food at all, was that Ali felt ostracised by Ibrahim. One day, having been chased away from his family, Ali sat on some rocks overlooking the vast desert and looked soulfully back in the direction of Ur from whence he had left years earlier.

Ali liked this time of day. The sun didn't sear down on him as much, for which he was grateful to Allah. Ali enjoyed the peace, the solitude and the gentle breeze on his face. He felt the cicadas chirped a cheery song just for him. A cicada even landed in his open palm as he sat, mouth open, staring into the desert. Then a wonderful idea burst forth into Ali's mind. He closed his hand into a fist, and quickly slipped the cicada into his mouth. He praised Allah for His blessing, and In sha Allah, Ali would never have to be hungry again.

In Ur, the imam had wanted Ibrahim's land. Although Ibrahim's land was barren, barely able to sustain a few goats, the imam amassed significant wealth by advising poor Shia farmers to migrate west. When Ibrahim reached the straits on the coast of Anatolia, south of the Sea of Marmara, he was too frail to continue; and considered this is where the imam intended him to settle. Ibrahim discovered that life was no better than in Ur. Life for Ali was worse.

One early evening, whilst Ali was banished to the rocks, a camel train approached him. Some friendly Arabs waved.

"*As-Salamu-Aleikum*," said the cameleers.

"*Wa-Aleikum-Salaam*," Ali excitedly exclaimed, rushing up to them. The Shia cameleers' greeting Ali like a little brother, tethered the camels laden with tents and heavy equipment near the rocks. One of them, searching a bag hanging from his camel, produced some dates and gave them to Ali. Some men, Ali did not recognise as Arab, wearing loose-fitting Arab clothes, their heads covered by traditional kufiya, approached Ali.

"Hallo, *As-Salamu-Aleikum*," the nearest one said, cordially extending his hand.

Ali did not understand the German Hallo, but responded with an excited, "*Wa-Alaikum-Salaam.*"

The men sat with Ali, who enjoyed their attention. The cameleers unburdened the camels from their heavy equipment and began to set up camp. One of the men, telling Ali, he was a German missionary, gave him a book, for which Ali expressed his gratitude by saying, "Shukran," and performing a little bow.

The Bible gave Ali great comfort, cushioning him as he sat on it, on the rocks, talking with his new friends. The missionaries' Arabic sounded strange, interspersed with strange German phrases, which at that stage Ali did not understand.

Ali pointed to the direction of Ur from whence as a small boy; he had walked, as he tried to describe the ancient geological features of the landscape. The men politely refused a cicada, which Ali caught for them. One of the Germans offered Ali a delicious sickly-sweet drink, which they all shared together. The men described partly in Arabic, partly in German and partly with their hands how the nice drink would help Ali better describe the geological formations, he had encountered on his journey from Ur to Çanakkale. Ali was feeling loquacious; gesticulating, gawping and laughing amongst his new friends. The delicious drink was schnapps.

The Germans did not disclose to Ali what they were doing in Çanakkale, but they were not missionaries. They empathised with Ali, saying they had also come from afar, in the direction, from which Ali had been pointing. They did not disclose they were one of several German exploratory parties that had been sent to ensure the completion of the Berlin to Baghdad railway, to transport petroleum to fuel Germany's rapidly expanding economy.

In 1901, German geologists reported vast supplies of petroleum around the Tigris and Euphrates; and construction of the Berlin to Baghdad railway began shortly thereafter. However, German engineers, who had encountered difficulties tunnelling through the Taurus Mountains, left the railway incomplete. Senior geologist, Dr Helmut Berenger was a distant relation of Wilhelm Berenger, Blumberg Barrister, (but this was unknown to either party).

Dr Berenger and his party had been sent by Kaiser Wilhelm II, German Emperor and King of Prussia on a matter of national significance. The Berlin to Baghdad railway must be completed at all costs. Ali would have understood none of this and believed that the Germans were missionaries. After they had fed Ali, and gave him some dates and supplies to bring to his family, Ali promised to return the next day.

The next morning as the sun rose and the three cameleers were performing their morning prayers, Dr Berenger saw Ali and three men performing the same ritual some hundred yards away. The sun began to warm the chill morning. When the four guests arrived the three cameleers waited on them; the cameleers were courteous and especially respectful of Ibrahim due to his advanced years. Ibrahim looked very old indeed. Welcoming Ibrahim and inviting him to sit; his emotions overwhelmed him when the cameleers told them news of Ur. Ali felt excited; he had finally contributed to feeding his family. The two elder boys were reticent but very grateful to the cameleers.

Two Berber tents had been erected in an 'L' shape to capture the morning sun. Ibrahim and his family waited patiently for Dr Berenger, enjoying the company and conversation of the three cameleers. When Dr Berenger appeared, he bowed to Ibrahim. Ibrahim stood to speak, physically supported by his two elder sons, Mohammad and Hussein, who sat at his feet. Ibrahim told Dr Berenger of their difficult life. He said when Ali was born, his wife, Fatima died. The imam said his wife died because Ibrahim loved Fatima more than he loved Allah; and now Ibrahim would not be accepted into paradise.

The imam told Ibrahim, Ali's disability was a curse from Shaitan and Ali must die too. Ibrahim looked at Ali and began to cry. Ibrahim told Dr Berenger, every time he rejected Ali, Ali would return to them spiritually stronger. This would further weaken their diminishing hope and resolve. Ali's brothers looked sullen. Ibrahim said the imam told Mohammad and Hussein: if they protected Ali, they would go to hell. Tears streamed down the cracks in Ibrahim's face during his confession. The tears dripped from Ibrahim's craggy chin onto the ground and disappeared in the sand.

Ibrahim cried for Mohammad, and cried for Hussein and cried most bitterly for Ali. Ibrahim said he had seen Mohammad and Hussein ridicule Ali in front of his face, then profusely apologise when Ibrahim was not looking. Ibrahim knew that

47

sometimes Mohammad and Hussein gave their food to Ali against God's will; and now there would be no one to speak for them of the Day of Judgment.

"I will speak for them, father," said Ali, interrupting.

"I will speak for you too."

Ali offered Ibrahim a cicada, and Ibrahim fell at his son's feet in contrition.

Dr Berenger and the scientists waited patiently for Ibrahim to compose himself.

Finally Dr Berenger stood up and said, "*Bismillah al-rahman al-rahim* (In the name of God, the Most Gracious, the Most Merciful)."

"Ibrahim, you are a wise man. We would like to help you and your family. Your son, Ali speaks highly of you all. You have been welcomed as guests and you are welcome to remain as long as we are here."

Dr Berenger then sat down with his colleagues and discussed something in German.

He beckoned Mohammad, Hussein and Ali to approach and spoke in broken Arabic and some German, "We would like you to assist us in our project. We would like you to report to us any persons coming through the area as we have some important work to conduct."

"Of course, we will feed you all and the cameleers will take care of Ibrahim whilst you remain with us. Are you able to do this?"

Mohammad nodded, and kissed Dr Berenger on the hand. Hussein followed his elder brother and Ali gave Dr Berenger and open-mouthed vacant look.

As the little camp was near the coast, the young men decided the following day, Hussein, would construct his lookout about a mile south of the camp because that was the least dangerous of the two positions; and Mohammad, watching over Ali, would construct his lookout about a mile north. If there was any suspicious movement in the north, Mohammad would return to camp to report to Dr Berenger and send Ali to collect Hussein.

If Hussein saw suspicious movement in the south, he would return to camp and report to Dr Berenger. They would meet at the rocks for their midday meal to discuss if any strangers passed through the area and return to their lookout positions until dusk, whereupon they would return to their camp.

The evenings were very enjoyable for Ali. He liked the company at the camp and despite his intellectual difficulties; he appeared to be learning German well. He deeply respected Dr Berenger as Ali had never before been treated like a human being. Eventually, Ali was able to deliver daily situation reports in broken German. Ali began to translate for Hussein as well; both brothers holding Ali in admiration for his newly learnt skills.

Dr Berenger was kind and patient with Ali. Ali knew almost nothing about the world, so in the evenings Dr Berenger, without disclosing the reason why the German scientists were interested in Çanakkale, told the boys about his family in Prussia and how some of his grandfather's cousins had immigrated to South Australia: Lutheran migrants, who landed in 1838.

After about two months of very quiet activity, Hussein waited at the rocks for his midday meal with Mohammad and Ali, but neither of them appeared. Hussein waited until the sun was well past its apogee before approaching the copse of trees that Mohammad had selected as his lookout. There was no trace of either of them. A feeling of dread overcame Hussein and he ran back to report to Dr Berenger.

***

During the Balkan Wars, the Ottoman Empire, 'the Sick Man of Europe' suffered severely; losing most of its European territory. Losses described in military terms whereby, every Ottoman infantry regiment had been reduced by a battalion and every battalion had been reduced by a company. Mohammad and Ali had seen an old Jewish peddler with a horse and cart travelling between villages; but not before the old Jew had seen them the previous two days in a row, as they left their lookout to return to the rocks to meet Hussein. The old Jew had, for a modest fee informed the soldiers in the nearest village of their whereabouts. The cart appeared to have been laden with wares destined for the market.

The old Jew stopped his cart, erected a large bright parasol and sat calmly in the shade drinking tea. Mohammad and Ali had been enticed by the bright parasol and the prospect of tea to approach the Jew. A giant Turkish soldier popped up out of the cart and snatched them. Mohammad and Ali had been press-ganged into the 57th Turkish Infantry Regiment. It was the end of February 1915.

Holding the British equivalent rank of sergeant, Tolga was enormous. He weighed over 350 lbs. Tolga's cruelty and sadism knew no bounds. He had survived the Battle of Sarıkamış in the bitter Caucasus winter by resorting to cannibalism. Tolga was originally disgusted with himself when he first tasted human flesh to satiate his hunger. But he began to rejoice in eating the hearts of Russian prisoners before their petrified comrades, more for sensing the revulsion of his own comrades, than for his ever-increasing desire to feed his stomach. Tolga was feared and reviled, to which he delighted in his recognition and feeling of self-importance. When rumours of Tolga's outlandish behaviour reached his adjutant, Tolga's comrades were relieved he was sent to the newly established 57th Infantry Regiment in Çanakkale.

Tolga picked up Mohammad by the face, with one giant hand and threw him into the peddler's cart. He looked at Ali, who stood trembling, mouth agape. As Tolga reached over the cart and put his enormous hand on Ali's face, Ali began to urinate. Tolga lifted Ali by the neck, up over his head and whilst doing so Ali's urine struck Tolga in the face.

Enraged, Tolga hurled Ali down into the cart. Preparing to smash Ali's head, Tolga heard the old Jew shout, "Dur!" (Stop!)

The new recruits, bundled into the cart, were taken north by the old Jew to the Hellespont for transportation across the straits to Maidos; and further to reinforce the 57th Regiment stationed at Arı Burnu.

The old Jew thought about the coins, he would receive jingling merrily in his pocket from two Arab recruits rather than one. As the little cart bumped over the stony track, Tolga sat opposite Ali, eating something supplied by the old Jew, which turned out to be pork.

Upon arrival at the Hellespont, the old Jew received his booty and disappeared with the horse and cart. Bustling with troops and stores destined to cross to Maidos in European Çanakkale, Ali and Mohammad were manhandled onto a troop transport vessel. Not being able to communicate well in Turkish,

Mohammad found himself squeezed up against another Arab. The man, an Arab Nationalist, had not volunteered to serve in the Ottoman Army but had been recruited in the same manner as Mohammad and Ali.

Observing Mohammad's ethnicity, the man grumbled that this business was not Arab business. He did not believe that Kaiser Wilhelm had converted to Islam.

"The Turks are fools," he spat.

"If the Germans win the war, the Turks will only ever be second rate Germans. If the Germans lose the war, the Turks will lose everything."

"The Grand Mufti of Istanbul has declared jihad upon the British. But the Grand Mufti's jihad is a Sunni jihad. We Shia will not find emancipation by dying for the Sunni," the Arab reasoned.

He whispered to Mohammad and Ali that if they ever wanted to see their family again, they had best learn from him the subtle art of sabotage.

They three sat together next to the unreliable engine of the troop transport, the noise of which, dissuaded any other passenger to enjoin their Arab conspiracy. The Arab, whose identity remained unknown to Mohammad and Ali, considered nobody else spoke Arabic aboard the troop transport. He became a little more candid in his conversation with his newly found Arab co-conspirators. In order to discourage unwanted attention, he began to discuss in Arabic how to disable the troop transport's engine. His muffled guffaw when the engine spluttered and stopped on its own accord about halfway across the channel was not missed by Tolga.

Whilst the troop transport casually drifted in the direction of the Aegean Sea, to the abuse of the boatmen by Tolga to fix the engine. The Arab confided with Mohammad and Ali that he knew someone, who been in touch with a British agent. If the British win the war, the British will ensure Arab independence from both the Germans and the Turks.

The troop transport catching the strong current of the Narrows drifted through the night many miles past their original destination. Mohammad and Ali drifted off to sleep whilst the troop transport merrily drifted towards the Aegean Sea. Tolga verbally abused every passer by he could see on-shore in a rescue attempt, which was accordingly ignored.

Chapter 6
Retribution

"If you wait by the river long enough, the body of your enemy will float by."

Sun Tzu

Tolga's hapless troop transport was intercepted by the Nusret, a Turkish mine-laying vessel; harsh words were exchanged between the Nusret's Master and Tolga, who felt humiliated before his recruits assembled ashore. Tolga estimated at least two full days' march along the rough coastal track to reach Maidos. Ali, had already learnt a few Turkish phrases; most of them, the darkest of obscenities escaping from Tolga's foul mouth during their unintended wanderings in the Dardanelles towards the Aegean Sea.

Listening to Tolga cursing, whilst his heaving, sweating mass, waddled along, Ali was adding to his colourful repertoire of expletives. The journey had taken nearly 48 hours for the recruits; marching 20 hours per day and sleeping like the dead in the bushes, next to the track for four. The Arab, Mohammad and Ali met on the troop transport did not wake up on the first morning. He had died, strangled by Tolga as he slept during the night.

The recruits stopped to drink water from a stream trickling beneath a culvert into the sea. They had not eaten for two days. Ali was desperately thirsty; his mouth was dry, his lips cracked and his tongue swollen. Cool and crystal clear, the water from the stream, to him, tasted wonderful. In fact, it was brackish. Immersing his salt encrusted face in cupped handfuls, Ali praised Allah for His beneficence.

More Turkish obscenities from Tolga, and the recruits wearily pressed on. Tolga barged into several fishermen's homes along the way; took what food he wanted, assaulted the inhabitants if they did not supply him with provisions and continued on. At Fort Kilitbahir, the training officer, a German was waiting for Tolga with Tolga's new rank – corporal.

The German instructors at Fort Kilitbahir were meticulous in organising the influx of recruits. As well as the administration centre and stepping off point for Turkish battalions deploying to the peninsula, Fort Kilitbahir was also a recruit training camp. Instead of complementing experienced Turkish battalions with trained but inexperienced platoons piecemeal, the Germans organised a more efficient process; whereby a Turkish battalion would receive a basic-trained infantry company upon graduation.

The Turkish infantry battalions marched in to Maidos from the Hellespont. There was a modest official ceremony for the graduating Turkish company of recruits at Fort Kilitbahir, who paraded past the German Commanding Officer, Regimental Sergeant Major, German Training Officer and miscellaneous staff, directly into their battalions. The Turkish battalions immediately deployed with their new company in tow to military establishments along the peninsula.

The Regimental Sergeant Major at Fort Kilitbahir, was dissatisfied with the unsatisfactory standards the recruits had attained; as graduations had been scheduled like clockwork to occur on a monthly basis. Some platoons formed after their training had been officially scheduled to start, (such as Tolga's platoon); and graduated as the third, and lowest-rated platoon of a company of about 100 men. Ali, at the completion of his training would learn that he was the least competent soldier of the lowest-rated platoon of the 57th Infantry Regiment's graduating class, April 1915: a designation, he was not unhappy with.

In February 1915, the Regimental Sergeant Major discussed his concerns with the Commanding Officer: the Turkish recruit was not as enthusiastic as the recruits in his previous Prussian command. He was resilient if given the appropriate training and guidance. The Regimental Sergeant Major added with concern, the Arab recruits were equally resilient, but they were devious, and unreliable if not monitored closely. This counsel was not lost on the wizened Commanding Officer. The Regimental Sergeant Major wielded a strong influence with the Commanding Officer, who was under pressure from Constantinople to produce increasing numbers of trained soldiers to reinforce Turkish regiments. Battalions flooded in from their brigade training exercises in Asian Çanakkale.

Upon arrival at Fort Kilitbahir, Tolga's exhausted recruits were fed and allowed to retire to their barracks, whilst Tolga was sent 'to have coffee' with the Commanding Officer. On the parade ground, after breakfast the following morning, the Training Officer made a speech, which only Mohammad and Ali were able to decipher. The Turkish junior instructors, shouted at the recruits to stand at attention, whilst they saluted the German Training Officer before he left. Followed by a lot more shouting, pushing and shoving, the recruits were ushered into a large training hall, where they were individually interviewed in a various number of languages.

As not one of the recruits could read, they were invited to sign an 'X' next to their name, at the bottom of a number of documents, which were secured in the machinery of the German administration system.

The Turkish junior instructors then shouted at the recruits some more, pushed and shoved them outside and formed them into three platoons of three files, approximately 30 recruits per platoon. Ali heard a familiar Turkish voice. Turkish obscenities arose from a sanitation trench, parallel to the parade ground, extending from the ablution block. The trench had been uncovered and was being enlarged to cope with the increasing number soldiers and recruits passing through Fort Kilitbahir.

At the bottom of the trench laboured Tolga. The large effluence pipe had been temporarily boarded up whilst Tolga hacked away at sides of the trench to enlarge the narrow channel. He did not look up as the recruits marched past. But Tolga could observe a few disdainful looks from over the crest, in the reflection of one of the small pools of liquid sewerage that was left to coagulate in the sun after the effluent had been blocked off at the source. The recruits' inquisitive scrutiny infuriated him, so Tolga started to devise a plan to seek retribution against them, and his German masters, who had sentenced him to the trench. Tolga would make a bomb.

A Turkish drill instructor marched Ali's platoon to another large building, which housed the quartermaster's store. They were issued: a khaki tunic each, two shirts, two pairs of trousers, a belt, a Wolseley-pattern-cork-helmet, dressed in Turkish style – a başlık, (not to be worn by recruits under training), two pairs of socks and puttees without boots. Ali, who had no shoes, was clubbed around the ear by a Turkish instructor, who saw Ali put a pair of socks on his hands.

This activity lasted until about noon, whereupon the recruits marched back to Fort Kilitbahir soldiers' mess; passing Tolga labouring away. Tolga's enormous head protruded at about ankle height from the trench, hands on hips, truculently attempting to make eye contact with them. He was ignored. Day-in, day-out, the recruits were drilled, marching past Tolga, who sometimes rested the handle-end of his shovel into the flesh of his chest, looking ever more resentful out of his new domain.

One afternoon, several recruits including Mohammad and Ali were instructed to run to the quartermaster's store to uplift their boots, which had recently arrived. When they entered the quartermaster's store they saw the old Jew stuffing his pockets with brass buttons and buckles. The old Jew, who also saw Mohammad and Ali advancing upon him, shrank into a corner behind a long counter; brass buttons falling from his pockets as he did so, as Turkish insults were hurled at him.

To the old Jew's back was a long, high shelving system, which stocked trousers, shirts, bins for socks, separate bins for puttees, belts and all manner of kit, which the recruits had been not yet issued. The door to the quartermaster's store was between the old Jew and his attackers. The window, which was within the Jew's reach, had been nailed shut to prevent thieves from entering the store. The old Jew crouched on the floor and resigned himself to a beating.

Fate intervened by a Turkish fist punching Mohammad to the side of his face, dropping him sprawling to the ground. The other recruits stood to attention in one rank; dressing by the right, arms at their sides, heels together, chin-up, eyes to the front.

The old Jew spotted his chance.

"Onbaşı, (corporal), I have boots for these men," he said as he brushed himself off and slipped the Turk a cigarette with an obsequious smile.

The Turkish instructor went outside and waited for the men to be issued their boots.

Avraham: merchant, part-time free-lance recruiter for the 57th Infantry Regiment, Ottoman Army; usurer and Jew, had added assistant commissariat at Fort Kilitbahir to his curriculum vitae. As a Jew, Avraham was exempt from service in the Ottoman Army, but he was charged a tax for not being Muslim, which Avraham thought both outrageous and extortionate.

Sensing their revulsion, Avraham (who had embarked on the business of procuring boots, brass buttons, buckles and miscellaneous military equipment to resell back to the Ottoman army), decided to confide some information to Mohammad and Ali in order to deflect their loathing of him onto someone else.

First, Avraham advised them he had heard a rumour that the British and French would attempt to seize the straits on the 18 March. Whispering very softly now, he slipped Ali a map of the Gallipoli peninsula and inquired whether they would be interested in working privately for him on a part-time basis, collecting 'abandoned' military equipment, starting from today.

With crocodile tears welling-up in his eyes, Avraham said in a whining voice that Tolga had coerced him on threat of death to carry out the deception in the desert to press-gang them, (which was true). Avraham omitted to disclose, he had already engaged in an arrangement with the Training Officer to deliver prospective recruits from Asian Çanakkale to the Hellespont for transportation to Fort Kilitbahir.

In the evening when Ali was relieving himself in the dark outside the ablution block, which was temporarily out of bounds, he thought about the subtle art of sabotage, and the Arab assassinated by Tolga. The large effluence pipe, which protruded from beneath the ablution block, had been manually closed from the inside by turning a large valve controlling effluence from within. The ablution block was about 30 yards long; as was the length of the effluence pipe, but which protruded from the block by a little less than a foot; inclined downwards at about 45 degrees, allowing sewerage to flow into a large barrel dug into the sanitation trench; the barrel sat next to four other barrels stored in a row.

The four barrels would be transported simultaneously by horse and cart for their contents to be burnt when four out of the five were full; the fifth being left to capture the sewerage produced on the day, the remaining barrels were taken. Overflow formed in puddles in the bottom of the trench; the obnoxious stench was currently being addressed by a German engineer.

Boards had been nailed to cover the effluence pipe to prevent vermin from crawling inside. Burning the sewerage was conducted once a week, by recruits on punishment detail; supervised by an instructor, also on punishment detail. In the absence of any recruits available to be punished, Tolga had been sentenced to complete the task by himself. Ali released the valve causing sticky warm sewerage to build-up and press against the boards. The weather had been decidedly hot this week, and the methane and toxic gases, caused by the build-up of sewerage was ready to explode. Ali slipped back into his barracks and crept into bed whilst the sewerage was left to gradually build up against the boards sealing it in.

The next day, as the sun scorched down upon Fort Kilitbahir, the recruits' lunch was interrupted by a large explosion at the ablution block. Recruits dived for cover under their tables as the Turkish instructors ran to the mess windows to see what had happened. They saw other Turkish instructors cautiously appear at the windows of other buildings at the compound. A whole platoon and their drill instructor had run from the parade ground and taken cover behind the quartermaster's store.

The Regimental Sergeant Major, angrily peering through his office window, and observing pieces of excrement covered board strewn across his beloved parade ground was livid. He marched over to the site of the explosion. The detonation had caused a violent torrent of sewerage to spew forth, confined by the high walls of the trench encasing everything in its path with putrid sludge.

Unfortunately for Tolga, he was labouring only a few feet from the centre of the detonation. He had been blown some way back down the trench and was presently, on his back, winded, cursing, swimming in sewerage and struggling to get up. The Regimental Sergeant Major called over the Turkish instructors, who called over the recruits from the mess hall. The recruits had some difficulty extracting giant Tolga from the trench, whose irascibility caused them to drop him back into the sludge. Ali stood victorious at the crest of the trench and even assisted in dropping Tolga back in.

Tolga could hardly bare the humiliation. Completely undermining his fearful reputation, he knew the incident would become the source of great mirth and legend in the recruits' barracks; and the instructors' office as they disingenuously frowned at Tolga's predicament. However, when Tolga appeared 'for coffee' with the German Training Officer in the afternoon, the Training Officer was not amused.

Tolga was blamed for the explosion because he was too slow in completing the trench. Had he completed the trench, in a timely fashion, the valve could have been released accordingly without causing the explosion. The Training Officer immediately sent newly demoted private Tolga to Ari Burnu to join the 57th Regiment's machine gun company. Recruit training was interrupted for all platoons when they were required by the Commanding Officer to assist in fortifying the guns at Fort Mecidiye. It was 16 March.

***

Seyit was a tough, resilient soldier, who had served in the Balkans Wars. He was a hard worker but not yet an instructor. Mohammad, Ali and the recruit platoon had been seconded to Seyit's charge to complete the defences at Fort Mecidiye pending an imminent attack, which had been kept secret from the platoon and from Seyit.

The ammunition stores at Fort Mecidiye had been constructed of masonry and their rooves had been constructed of steel metal arches. To reinforce the ammunition store in case of an explosion, earth had been built up along the sides and on top of the store. The earth works had as yet been unfinished and Seyit was given one concise instruction from his sergeant, repeatedly with increased urgency throughout the day, "Çabuk ol!" (Hurry up!)

The stores provided ammunition for the heavy guns covering the straights. There were two sets of doors, one at each end of the ammunition stores: one for the ammunition to be off-loaded from transport carts at the rear of the store and the other, for ammunition to be fed to the guns at the front, facing the sea.

The platoon was scheduled to work 24 hours per day in three shifts until the task was completed with two sections working at any one time and one section stood down to rest. The ammunition weighing over 600lbs per shell was fed mechanically into the guns. The section, which had been stood down to rest would eat and rest in the gun emplacement itself.

Ali watched with great interest as the Turkish gunners cleaned and maintained the gun and the mechanical feeder during the day. When the gunners finished, they went to dinner. The gunners were permitted to go to the battery mess to eat. The recruits were not. Food was brought to them so they could carry on working. The Turkish gunners left some maintenance tools stored at the site: screwdrivers, spanners, a hammer, a large mallet and a large container of oil.

Ali secreted a spanner into his tunic. In evening, when his section were asleep and the other two sections were working piling earth on top of the ammunition store, Ali crept under the mechanical ammunition feeder-tray loosening the nuts securing the tray to its frame, so it would fall off when operated. Unconsciously, a new facial expression entered Ali's hitherto limited repertoire.

When Ali undertook a task requiring intellectual computation, Ali's tongue would twist and protrude rudely from his mouth especially where the task required some technical physical effort such as the one he had presently embarked upon. When completed, Ali secreted the spanner back with the stored tools and quietly stole back to where Mohammad was sleeping.

The next morning as Mohammad and Ali were busy piling earth on top of the ammunition store, Mohammad looked up to see warships ominously sailing up the straits from the Aegean. In a panic, Mohammad ran down to Seyit, who was supervising work inside the Ammunition store. The ships had been seen and reports followed their progress from Cape Hellas. The Turkish gunners were instructed by their officers to make ready their guns and await further instructions.

The recruits were pushed and shoved into the ammunition stores to be ready to clear debris if the emplacements were hit by the ships' guns. At 11:00 am, a massive explosion rocked Ali's ammunition store as the guns of the French ship *Gaulois* began pounding the Fort, followed by the guns of HMS *Queen Elizabeth* and HMS *Vengeance*. Ali's nose and ears began to bleed. The Turkish gunners began to fire back, striking the *Gaulios* with their first round.

Upon the gunnery officer's command to reload, the ammunition feeder-tray fell off. Turkish gun emplacement No. 3 was disabled, and the gunners looked dumbfounded at their officer; as panic was about to set in. Plucky little Seyit picked up a 600lb shell and blood pouring from his nose, began to make his way up the steps to the Turkish gun.

A second hit on the *Gaulios* was responded to in kind by a hit on the emplacement killing several of the gunners but not Seyit, who had returned into the ammunition store to retrieve another shell. The recruits were now required to remove the gunners' mangled bodies, clear the debris and replace the dead gunners. The Turkish officer, whose leg had been severed, continued to issue orders to the gun crew for the second round to be fired; whereupon he died.

Suffering concussion from the constant bombardment, all the recruits looked to Seyit to take command amongst the dust and rubble. The Turkish gun was aimed directly at the *Gaulios*, claiming a third direct hit.

Turkish eyes had previously observed from Asian Çanakkale, British and French ships turn to starboard as they entered and left Erin Kőy Bay near the mouth of the straits. The Turkish minelayer, Nusret had discretely laid mines along the Asian shore to capture just such a manoeuvre.

Despite the clear water at Erin Kőy Bay, a British spotter-plane locating mines placed across the straits further up at the Narrows, failed to locate the mines parallel to the Asian shore. Mines had been located by a civilian trawler in a previously cleared area, but reports had not been transmitted to the captain of the French ship *Bouvet*, which capsizing upon striking a mine, sank in a few minutes. The attack on the straits was a disaster: the French *Bouvet* sunk, the *Gaulios* and *Suffren* severely damaged; the British HMS *Irresistible* and HMS *Ocean* sunk, and the HMS *Inflexible* severely damaged. Dead sailors returned blackened and carbonised upon mangled decks.

The significance of this event was lost on Ali as he lay almost unconscious amongst the rubble face down in the ammunition store. Some recruits lay dead, missing body parts; others savagely wounded cried for help. Seyit dazed and unsteady attempted to continue his duties.

Mohammad and Ali were sent back to the military hospital at Maidos where they recovered to graduate with the recruit class of 1 April 1915; and were immediately sent to the 57th Regiment's machine gun company at Ari Burnu. Divisional Commander Mustapha Kemal visited his new soldiers formed on the company parade ground.

Keeping his disappointment to himself as he passed between the ranks, he stopped to chat. Upon inspecting the third and final rank, of the third platoon, a concerned expression had come over his face. As he made eye contact with the Arab soldier, at the far end of the final rank, gawping at him with his mouth open, Mustapha Kemal sighed and his shoulders sank.

Chapter 7
Insanity

"I don't order you to fight, I order you to die. In the time it takes us to die, other troops and commanders can come and take our places."

Mustapha Kemal

Tolga was from Constantinople. The streets were often devoid of respectable females. Tolga's mother and other like-minded women lived by their wits; suggestively standing in the dark alcove of their crowded back-street boudoir. The boudoir was presided over by an obese woman with a dusky voice and a strong pair of hands. She was Tolga's father. Men showed more than a passing interest in chubby Tolga, as he looked innocently out at the world, clinging to his mother's chemise. He too was introduced to living by his wits. Tolga soon ran away.

Tolga was caught stealing food in the Grand Bazaar. Before Tolga suffered a beating from the aggrieved hawker, an old bookseller from a nearby stall paid for the food and apologised on Tolga's behalf. The bookseller was held in high esteem by the merchants and dealers in his corner of the bazaar. Although the hawker could have exaggerated the offence and asked for more compensation, he was satisfied with cuffing little Tolga around the head, whilst the old bookseller wasn't looking.

Mehmet, the old bookseller, with a gradually decrementing spine unnaturally stooped, asked Tolga whether he would like to assist him working in his bookstall. Tolga, already an emotionally damaged boy, was thinking about stealing the old man's money before running away. They threaded their way back through the throng; Mehmet grasping onto Tolga's reluctant arm, at which time Tolga realised the question was rhetorical.

The bookstall, an eight by six-foot space, which doubled as Mehmet's compact but comfortable dwelling, rested astride two similar bookstalls in the Grand Bazaar; whose proprietors, their interest piqued, stole inquisitive looks at the incongruous pair as the old bookseller approached with their new neighbour. Beneath the shutters, two cushions congenially sat either side of a low round table, which had seen many cups of Turkish coffee; the residue of circles upon circles of coffee stains, quietly revealing the approximate number if not the nature of the discussions, which had been held around it.

Shuttered in the evenings, the little bookstall's shelving stood floor to ceiling against the walls; the Qur'an occupying the most prestigious place on the top shelves. Ornate but worn Turkish rugs covered the floor. An independent wooden box tucked away in a corner contained all of the old man's worldly possessions. At first glance, Tolga thought this was where Mehmet, the old bookseller kept his money.

Tolga was required to keep an eye on the bookstall when Mehmet curled up on the floor beneath one of the rugs in the afternoons to go to sleep; a task Tolga did not find too onerous. By Tolga's sullen expressions, confronting glances, surly posture, lips pursed and arms crossed; Mehmet was unsurprised that no books were sold, whilst he was sleeping.

Customers coming to Mehmet to talk about Islam or philosophy over tea or Turkish coffee; became oblivious to the noise, the overwhelming colours, exotic smells of spices, and the busy hubbub of vendors, purchasers, browsers and street-urchins, whose snake-like hands pilfered the pockets of the unwary. Some customers came to tell Mehmet about their problems: the dissatisfaction in their search for love, their dysfunctional families, the extortionate tax they were required to pay, the price of fish or just the weather, (the latter would be a euphemism that the customer wished to enter into a discussion about the dissatisfaction in their search for love).

Mehmet, quietly listening, displayed the patience of Job and the wisdom Solomon. Compassionate with his customers, Mehmet would sometimes pat them on the arm in an avuncular fashion. A book was purchased, even by the illiterate for Mehmet's wise counsel. As Tolga lay curled up on the mat, he felt Mehmet's words begin to sooth him as he fell asleep.

Mehmet had been a dervish and an ascetic in the desert. He possessed the intellect of a Sunni scholar but Mehmet's eyes had begun to fail him. He talked to himself and often forgot where he put the coffee pot with the worn handle.

Tolga had rescued the coffee pot one day as it wound its way through the throng in the impish hands of a street urchin. Although Mehmet had become absent-minded, he had an immense memory and argued out loud with himself about the meaning of certain passages of the Qur'an.

When Mehmet was a young man, he had been a Mevlevi acolyte. Intensely desiring a personal relationship with Allah, he learnt to perform the intricate sequence of dervish steps to achieve religious ecstasy. Raising his hands in submission, one hand palm-up, one hand palm-down, his head inclined, his expression serene, Mehmet entered a swirling state: the white gown, black cloak, the tall brown sikke, balanced on his head, all symbols of mortality. From the rhythmic circular rotations and the centrifugal forces, Mehmet felt his soul leave his body.

First, Mehmet could look down upon himself whirling. He could look down upon the dervishes whirling around him until they became distant and insignificant. Then Mehmet was able to look down upon the Hagia Sophia until the minarets became fine needles and disappeared. Mehmet could see Ottoman villages and cities diminish into nothing. Further and further Mehmet's soul ascended into the heavens until even the blue-white earth became a speck and vanished into the night.

In his trance, Mehmet searched for Allah. Sometimes he sensed Allah's presence and sometimes he did not. Unable to abandon his desires, Allah was always beyond Mehmet's grasp. When finally Mehmet had ascended to where even the stars and galaxies disappeared, all that was left was a cold, dark emptiness. Mehmet experienced bliss in achieving this state; but as he eventually learned, the blissful state, however long, was always finite and never blissful at either end of his spiritual journey. Mehmet always felt having descended back into his body; a deep loneliness and disappointment pervade his consciousness until he awoke amongst friends, holding him steady by the arm.

Ultimately, Mehmet wondered whether the act of whirling was worthy or futile. In whirling, anticipation at the beginning was always tempered by the disappointment of returning into his body at the end. One day, when Mehmet was already a middle-aged man, he tripped over his gown, colliding with the other dervishes; causing a commotion. Mehmet was asked if he might consider studying to become a Muslim scholar.

After many years of recitation Mehmet memorised the complete Qur'an. He had become fastidious about completing the proper religious observations, rituals and ablutions in the correct order, with the appropriate religious intent. Once when offered a piece of watermelon, he respectfully declined because he could not recall any instance of the prophet Muhammad eating watermelon himself. His observation of ritual became so intense that Mehmet found the practice of ritual had become the object of worship.

Mehmet thought in circles; and thought about circles. He thought that if he set off on a journey west, and walked in a straight line, eventually, after years and years of walking, he would come back to the same place from whence his journey originated, but from the east.

He wondered whether space and time were bent into an enormous sphere forever whirling faster and faster at the periphery; like his billowing gown as he danced. As Mehmet had never reached the centre of the universe where time stood still, he thought his meditations were always constrained by time's passage.

Calculating if he waited long enough, through aeons upon aeons, eventually Mehmet would without physically moving from his cushions, coffee and low round table find himself back in the same space, from whence he had departed. Mehmet thought he had become learned but that he was not yet wise.

In order to further discipline his mind, Mehmet crossed into Asia and decided to live the contemplative life as cave dweller in Cappadocia. Water dripped from a crack in the ceiling of his cave; from the cave of the Gnostic, who lived above him. The Gnostic living above Mehmet complained that water dripped into his cave; from the cave of the Hasidic Jew, who lived above him. The domestic disputes between hermits, who lived above Mehmet as to the provenance of the leak began to drive Mehmet to distraction, so he returned to Constantinople.

Mehmet told Tolga that whirling only made him dizzy; study made him knowledgeable without insight, and asceticism made him, hungry, cold and lonely. Mehmet was happy with his humble bookstall in the bazaar; the comforts of the cushions, on which he sat over long conversations with heartbroken customers or distressed merchants. Mehmet realised in the scheme of things their problems were insignificant. But in the present time and space, the problems were significant to his customers, so Mehmet gave them his empathetic ear and kindly smile, which contributed to alleviating their suffering. This, Mehmet believed was a worthy raison d'être.

Mehmet knew, one day soon, he would die. He was unsure what would happen to him thereafter, but he but neither judged those, who firmly believed in an afterlife, nor judged those, who firmly believed there was not. Mehmet determined, in his present existence, he was content. One evening, after lowering the shutters at the bookstall, which muffled the noise of people in the bazaar rushing to and fro, Mehmet patted Tolga on the arm in an absent-minded way. A horrific memory of hands fondling him entered Tolga's mind. Tolga grabbed the coffee pot and beat Mehmet about the head until the old man was dead. Tolga slipped under the shutters and stole away into the night.

Despairing, Tolga some years later found himself in the Ottoman Army. With Mehmet's meagre earnings Tolga left the bustling port at Constantinople and sailed on a ferry to Maidos. At Fort Kilitbahir, Tolga was trained as an infantryman. His predilection for cruelty was noted when he was found torturing a cat, which gave birth to her litter under his barracks. The cat and the kittens all went into a sandbag, disappearing with Tolga through the gates at the Fort.

Tolga was discovered, late in the evening, by a sentry at the Fort bashing the bag repeatedly against the rocks on the seashore. When approached by the sentry, the mewing and screeching had not yet ceased but Tolga discarded the evidence by throwing the bag into the sea. A report was made to Tolga's adjutant; who transferred Tolga, as far away as possible, to the Ottoman 3rd Army in the northeastern frontier of the Ottoman Empire.

Tolga was immediately unpopular in his new regiment, and was accordingly shuffled around from company to company. Although he was the largest, most intimidating solider in any unit, into which he was deposited, Tolga maintained a realistic fear of his Non-Commissioned Officers. When Tolga fell asleep on sentry he was punished severely. When Tolga's weapon was found to be dirty, he spent a lot of time in the armoury cleaning weapons.

***

Armenia adopted Christianity in the fourth century. Kars Province was settled by Armenian Christians some of whom, served with the Armenian Volunteers in the Russian Army as a means to wrest Christian independence from Ottoman Islam. The Germans persuaded the leader of the Young Turk Revolution, Enver Pasha to open the Caucasian Front with Ottoman troops; to relieve the Germans fighting on the Eastern Front in Russia. Strategically, the Germans wanted to sever Russian access to oil reserves around the Caspian Sea.

By the time Tolga arrived at the foot of the Allahuekber Mountains it had already started to snow. With only dry bread and olives for rations, even Tolga, with his generous covering of body-fat began to feel bitterly cold. Perspiration, which trickled down the soldiers backs whilst on the march, began to freeze when they stopped to rest. Their attention began to waiver in the cold.

They were surprised by the Armenians, taking many unnecessary casualties in battle. However, the Ottoman Army overwhelmed the Armenian's by sheer weight of numbers. Tolga captured his first Russian prisoner. Completely lacking in any sense of discipline, Tolga beat the poor fellow to death before his terrified Russian comrades. The soldiers, who served with Tolga were so cold they merely looked on, pulling their collars up, shivering uncontrollably.

Unimpressed with their indifference, an enraged Tolga grabbed a second prisoner, and stripping him bare to the waist, stabbed him repeatedly in the chest. The helpless prisoner fell dead to the ground. Then reaching up through the prisoner's intestines Tolga withdrew his punctured heart, and raised it to the sky, blood dripping on Tolga's face. Looks of complete contempt at Tolga's macabre display dissipated as they looked away, cold numbing their emotions. In the dark, with maniacal eyes, Tolga began to eat.

His social castigation complete, Tolga sat disconsolate and dissatisfied in the snow; the dead prisoner at his feet. Tolga knew

Allah had created everything. Therefore, Allah had created War. Tolga wondered whether Allah could create a war so cruel and uncontrollable that not even Allah could control it. If Allah could, then War was greater than Allah. If Allah could not, then Allah could not create everything. Tolga received his answer in the morning.

War, Allah's creation had outgrown its creator. So cold was Tolga when he awoke, he was barely able to move. Brushing the snow from his tunic, Tolga realised, all around him had frozen to death.

***

Ali and Mohammad were relieved by a company of soldiers of another battalion of the 57th Regiment sent to reinforce the machine-gun company. Their argument outside the metal door of the concrete bunker had been whether they should remain to guard the imprisoned soldiers, or in the absence of Tolga, release them and tell Tolga, the prisoners had overwhelmed them and escaped.

Neither Mohammad nor Ali spoke English; nor did they know Berenger spoke German, but they were sure none of their prisoners spoke Arabic.

Mohammad said, "How can we be sure they will not kill us?"

As it turned out, Turkish reinforcements flooded into the compound. The commander of the reinforcements told Mohammad and Ali to return to their unit. So they ran to the track from whence the Turkish machine-gunners had left. Neither of them told the commander that Tolga did not trust them with ammunition so they were only issued with rifles without bayonets.

The track twisted beneath the barren escarpments between ridges, beyond which they could hear the constant *rat-a-tat-tat* of machine-gun fire. At a T-junction turning up the steep slope at the crest of which, was the Turkish machine-gun, they met more 57th Regiment reinforcements coming from the opposite direction also turning up the track. Scrambling to the Turkish trenches slightly forward of the summit, Mohammad and Ali continued along one branch of the trench to the sound of the guns, whilst the Turkish infantry fanned out along the other branch eventually leading to the high ground at Chunuk Bair.

As Mohammad and Ali crept along the last few yards towards the machine-gun, the gun went quiet. Tolga and a machine-gunner, ducking rifle fire ran towards them bent almost double. The two Turkish machine-gunners remained in position to hold the assault with rifle fire.

Just as the four were about to descend from the plateau, the Divisional Commander approached. Standing erect as bullets whizzed around them, he said sternly to Tolga, "Where are you going?"

"We have no ammunition left," Tolga lied.

He had ammunition in his rifle; only Mohammad and Ali, who had none issued, and the fourth soldier, who had given the remainder of his rifle ammunition to the soldiers at the machine-gun position, could honestly say that they had no ammunition.

Mustapha Kemal realising the urgency of the situation, knew that if the Turks lost the war, everything would be lost. He ordered them to lie down and face the enemy.

"I don't order you to fight, I order you to die. In the time it takes us to die, other troops and commanders can come and take our places," he said calmly.

Facing the enemy, the four Turkish soldiers lay down. The Australian attackers, charging up the slopes in pursuit, also lay down. Tolga cursing under his breath; Ali gawping at Tolga.

Chapter 8
Epiphany

The City

"But he attempted not the ascent courageously.
And what should make thee know what the ascent is?
It is the freeing of a slave.
Or feeding in a day of hunger
An orphan near of kin,
Or a poor man lying in the dust."

Noble Qur'an (90:12-17)

The grey metal cell-door swung open again, creaking on its hinges. Light filtered in around the silhouette of the giant Turk, as his hand clamped-down upon Berenger's face. Berenger forced the underside of his tongue up into the roof of his mouth, and pushed his chin down into his chest, to fend-off asphyxiation should the giant hand make its way to his throat. Kicking the feet of Faber and Cyril, the solicitor's clerk, they knew the signal was for them not to intervene.

Once outside, the hand was removed from his face. Berenger saw the dead soldier's battered body, tied to the cart by his feet. A macabre display designed to inspire fear and revulsion. It did neither. The soldier was dead: he could not feel pain. There was no point in reacting to the spectacle, in a manner that would have satisfied the giant Turk. Tolga had merely revealed he was an irrational sociopath. Therefore the giant Turk was weak: dangerous but weak.

Sergeant Berenger watched the two Arab soldiers in Turkish uniform nervously arrange the mangled body to its most dramatic effect. The Turkish soldiers, who had recently reinforced the compound, had fought the New Zealanders back to beyond the ridgeline dominating the encampment. Machine-gun fire could be heard in the distance.

Sergeant Berenger observed closely, one of the Arab soldiers of nervous demeanour, in the compound. A giant Turkish boot struck him on the leg and he fell to his knees.

"Mohammad!" Tolga growled.

Tolga pointed to the nervous soldier and then to some blindfolds, which had been laid over the side of the cart. The giant Turk had thus far given Berenger two names: 'Mohammad' and 'Ali'.

From his doting body language towards his Ali, Berenger inferred that Mohammad, somewhat facially similar to the first, was probably Ali's elder brother.

There was something else Berenger noticed about Mohammad. He appeared over-protective, in reaching across Ali and gathering the blindfolds. The gesture was not one to deflect the giant Turk's attention away from Ali, as Mohammad was the unfortunate focus of attention. Berenger determined he would make allies of Mohammad and Ali against the giant Turk by sundown.

Mohammad tied a blindfold around Berenger's face and tied his hands together behind his back. He clumsily searched Berenger's pockets whilst he was lying on his stomach and did not detect the pocket-watch. Berenger heard the creak of the grey metal door as it opened again. Since there were no ties on his legs, he knew they would be taken somewhere by foot.

One by one the prisoners were manhandled out of the bunker; blind-folded and thrown to the ground. Berenger heard them groan as their hands were bound. He rubbed his forehead into the ground in such a way that he could peer out of the bottom of his blindfold. He inclined his head slightly and espied gawping Ali; no magazine on his rifle, no bayonet. Ali stopped gawping and intently looked back. Ali did not report this to the giant Turk.

"Yes, an ally," Berenger whispered to himself.

Nine times the grey metal door creaked opened and shut. The final time, one of the two big Queenslanders was dragged out, kicking and struggling. Mohammad was head-butted. Several expletives later, followed by a whack from a giant hand; the Queenslander was on the ground. Tom Clarke, private soldier, 9th Queensland Battalion received a blind-fold wound tightly around his face and a rag thrust in his mouth, which was further bound with another rag around his face.

The giant Turk decided that Tom, as the prisoners' troublemaker would be leading the party behind Mohammad. Berenger was third in the order-of-march and the giant Turk was behind him. He expected Tom to try to escape soon, (and in his mind he wished Tom well, but Berenger thought he would be unsuccessful). Whilst Tom was causing problems for his guards, Berenger would kick the foot of one of the South Australians behind him, which would be the cue, to escape. Ali was likely to be guarding the rear.

They formed up in single file, as the sun began to set. Shuffling down the track, Tom, whom Sgt Berenger guessed could also see through his blindfold, bolted forward after pulling Mohammad to the ground. The giant Turk, brushing Berenger aside, strode after him. Cyril the solicitor's clerk was behind Berenger. Berenger turned and kicked Cyril's foot twice.

"Sergeant, I'm scared," was his reply.

"The Arab has no rounds in his rifle, no bayonet, and he is our ally," Berenger calmly said.

With that, Cyril, rubbed his forehead on Berenger's shirt lifting his blindfold and sprinted back up the track.

"Halt!" came Ali's nervous cry.

"*Alles ist gut*," Berenger said firmly.

A look of surprise from Ali; Cyril then head-butted him in the chest and he fell down. "*Ich heisse Wilhelm*," Berenger whispered.

"*Sprechen Sie Deutsche*, Ali?"

He nodded, amazed that Berenger knew the strange language in which he was familiar.

Before Berenger could say anything further, the giant Turk had turned around and fired a shot at Cyril, zigzagging up the track, but he missed.

"Everybody sit down!" Berenger shouted to the prisoners, some of whom were frantically trying to untie themselves and remove their blindfolds.

They, Berenger decided would not be so lucky in trying to escape. He also expected Tom to re-join them soon, as Tom had run down the track and not up it. As Berenger was soon to learn, within a hundred yards, Tom had run into further Turkish reinforcements making their way to Ari Burnu.

Their party was reduced to eight prisoners, and Tolga head-down, shoved and pushed them past the incoming Turkish soldiers. He had not concealed the body of the dismembered prisoner. Tolga knew that if he had been caught executing prisoners in such a way, instead of capturing them for intelligence value, he would have been shot.

"*Gitme!*" (Go) growled the giant Turk.

"Tolga," replied Mohammad fearfully.

Tolga. So that is his name, Berenger thought.

Tolga, head buried into his chest, smiled to himself, war had blessed him. The Turkish soldiers would not remember him as they rushed past in the fading light of the day. They may not even see the dead Australian as he lay in the half-light, he thought to himself. Tolga had escaped with murder yet again.

Sergeant Berenger paced five hundred yards over gradually descending ground, which undulated around the low ground. They came to a two-lane track crossing their path, where they stopped and Berenger listened. Endless reinforcements shuffled and stumbled south, presumably to Achi Baba.

As the prisoners staggered and slithered past them into the night, Berenger's binds began to eat into his wrists. He could hear the difference of boots hitting the ground as they moved from a dry-single track to a stony double-track. The sound of Turks marching the opposite direction into battle was more urgent. Berenger was unable to re-count how long the prisoners had been marching, hours or days.

Finally, in the cool air, Berenger could smell the sea. Then he heard a petrel and then another; and then they were on flat ground. Berenger could hear small waves lapping against a sea wall. They marched into a built-up area, the double-track turning to pavement. The squawking of seabirds, Turkish voices and the sound of stevedores unloading a vessel: they had reached a port. But they were jostled forward by Tolga, who struck one of the New Zealanders with the butt of his rifle.

A derogatory reply in a language, Berenger did not know, but guessed to be Māori was rewarded with a further thwack. They stopped. Berenger heard some muffled Turkish voices and a creak of large heavy doors opening. Pushed into a compound,

Berenger stood listening for some tell-tale sign of where they were. Some whispered voices: then he heard metal keys opening a metal gate.

A giant hand pushed him forward through the metal gates and down onto some stone stairs. Berenger smelt burning oil and he could see a naked flame from a torch through his blindfold as he gingerly made his way down; down the spiralling steps. With his right shoulder pressed against the cold masonry, Berenger continued to descend, until he heard muffled voices in Irish and Lancashire accents.

Some men were groaning. The prisoners made it to a stone landing, where they were instructed to remove their blindfolds and negotiated the remainder of the stairs aided by the intermittent flickering light of flaming torches.

They had descended about three full turns of stairs into a Byzantine dungeon. The architectural design of the dungeon appeared to be based on an underground cathedral. They were standing at one end of the dimly lit nave. On either side of the nave metal cages lined the walls. Contained within the metal cages, was a mass of prisoners separated by rank and location from where they were captured.

Beyond the transept at the intersection of the architectural cross, stood an imposing, heavy door concealing a suffocating ward in the ambulatory. To the right and left of the intersection of the transept were wide passageways.

Officers were separated from men. Those, who required more urgent medical attention were taken, or carried, through the heavy door and into the darkness at the end of the aisle. Faber, who had been shot through both hands, was taken away through the foetid air by a uniformed guard. He looked at Berenger in fear and pain as he was forcibly escorted away. Their number was down to seven.

They were handed over to the guard, one of whom unlocked an empty metal cage and pushed them in.

"No talking!" he growled in a heavy Turkish accent.

He locked the metal cage and returned to the bottom of the stairs dimly lit by candlelight, which Berenger had seen flickering beyond the doors at the near end of the nave. *That is the infirmary in the ambulatory*, he thought. He saw the guard through the open door of the office near the stairs from which they had descended. He hung the large ring of keys on the wall.

Each cage had a recently constructed stone barrier between them. This alone signified to Berenger that the assault upon Ari Burnu had been expected. At the front were metal bars, narrowly spaced, secured by the masonry at the floor and ceiling. Crossbars interspersed at such narrow intervals that even a small child would not be able to squeeze through. The construction was intended so prisoners could be observed. Berenger saw the guard sit at a makeshift desk; the guard's head nodded, bobbled and he fell asleep.

Sergeant Berenger determined that this place was sacred to early Christians but transformed into a prison by the Muslim Ottomans. The masonry on the walls appeared considerably newer than the masonry at the rear of the cell. In one back corner was a bucket of water: in the other back corner an empty bucket. The bucket was of a wooden type, waterproof and the slats were secured with a metal band near the rim and the base. A rope handle dangled from each. The roof rose to about eight foot above Berenger's head. He smelt vomit and urine. There was probably another floor above them but still below ground level.

"Men, I want you to dissemble the empty bucket: bend the metal bands back and forth until they break into lengths of about so. " Berenger showed how long with his hands.

"That is your cutting blade. You will make six cutting blades out of the two metal bands. With your cutting blade pare down the wooden slats into points, from which you will carve twelve wooden daggers. I will tie the rope handle into a monkey's fist and fashion it into a rope morning star. Give me the rivets securing the metal bands and I will insert them into the monkey's fist knot. Save all the shavings from the wooden slats and give them to me. I will need them to make a fire. We escape when our cell door is open. If I do not act, you will do nothing."

"But Sergeant…" A piercing glance and a stern frown at Tom in the dim light.

Tom knew he had already made one mistake. The next mistake he made could cost them their lives. Tom became silent. Many questions were fired in muffled whispers at Berenger from anxious soldiers gathered round, which he answered as thoroughly as he could. They diligently went about their instructions without further enquiry.

William, whose name Berenger later learnt was Wiremu, serving in the 3rd Auckland Infantry Regiment was Māori. Berenger had believed that Māori soldiers were forbidden to serve in white battalions, in accordance with Lord Kitchener's orders, originating as instructions for non-white colonials during the Boer War.

This fine specimen of a soldier, biceps bulging, popped the rivets securing the metal band to the wooden slats of the bucket with his bare fingers. He gave a white-toothed grin, discernible from the light at both ends of the nave; and gained the confidence of the rest of the men.

"You are second-in-command," Berenger quietly said, just loud enough for the others to hear.

"Psssst," Berenger heard from the cell next to his.

"Psssst, Private Patrick Kearney, Royal Munster Fusiliers."

"William," Berenger said, not wanting to give too much information to a stranger.

A distant pleasant memory of a conversation with a woman called Cornelia, years ago, in candle-lit canvas tent came to his mind; where he had divulged information without a concession from her. She had won a battle of wits.

"We were captured at Cape Hellas. Many killed in the landings. Our ship, the River Clyde grounded short of 'V' beach. We disembarked from large sally ports cut into the ship's hull but the Turkish machine-guns at Fort Sedd El Bahr had not been silenced by the bombardment this morning: tragedy, tragedy, dreadful tragedy."

Sergeant Berenger imagined a poorly planned romantic version of the Trojan horse, full of Irish soldiers waiting to be slaughtered, ill prepared for an assault on the beach.

"How many are you?" Berenger asked.

"Twelve," was the answer, confirming how many Berenger had counted.

I shall trust him just a little more, Berenger thought.

"*Psssst*, you. Are you there?" a voice from the other cell.

"Lance Corporal James Robert, 1st Battalion Lancashire Fusiliers."

There followed an equally tragic account of men cut to pieces on the barbed wire and the sea turning red with blood. Without a thought to the slain Englishmen, Berenger severely criticised their plan of assault in his mind. Berenger was yet to learn that six of their number had earned Victoria Crosses 'before breakfast' on W Beach at Cape Helles.

They were interrupted by the sound of tentative footsteps descending the stairs; the rattle of keys from the gaoler, who kept his keys with him, escorting another prisoner. The guard, who had awoken, removed the large ring of keys from the wall, and opened the gate to the dungeon. The guard from the top remained behind the gate and pushed the hapless prisoner through. His hands were tied behind his back, his blindfold pushed down around his neck. He looked to be injured as he shuffled in.

"Avustralya," Berenger heard a muffled voice say at the gate.

By the way this man moved, Berenger thought he recognised the prisoner but in the dim flickering light it was difficult to see. As the prisoner shuffled passed the candle-lit office, Berenger recognised a forlorn face – 'fat pants'. Staff-Sergeant Woolwich, quartermaster sergeant serving in the 10th South Australian infantry battalion. As Woolwich painfully made his way towards them, he sensed the tension in their cell mount.

He noted Wiremu's affable grin disappear. From his expression, the whites of his eyes, Berenger suspected that this morning was not the first time that Wiremu had killed a man. At this stage, they had not determined how to get from the dungeon up the stairs. Berenger's intention was to entice the top guard back down. He determined they would not attack as yet. He looked at Wiremu. Wiremu nodded. He looked at Tom. Tom looked disappointed.

The guard motioned for them to move to the rear of the cell. He did not notice that one of the buckets had been dissembled. Woolwich's eyes met Berenger's. He gave a look of surprise and tears started rolling down his cheeks. Pushed roughly into the cell. Woolwich stood back to the wall at the entrance and slid down. Sighing, his head and shoulders dropped.

"Carry on," Berenger whispered to the men.

The soft sound of sharpening blades being dragging across the stone floor continued.

Berenger approached Woolwich.

"William," Woolwich panted.

Sergeant Berenger checked his body for injuries. When he pushed his hand against Woolwich's shoulder, Woolwich emitted a weak moan. Berenger removed his hand covered in Woolwich's blood. He placed one of Woolwich's hands on his injury.

"Keep it there, Staff-Sergeant," Berenger said.

"Tell me how you got here and keep talking quietly until I tell you to stop."

Berenger carried on searching for further injuries.

"William, I've been shot."

"Do you have any other injuries?"

"No, but I'm so tired. William, William… I must tell you, when I landed, I did not have any rounds in my rifle or any in my ammunition pouches. I gave them all to you. I knew you and your men were landing before me so I gave them all to you because I knew you would be disembarking in the first wave. The rounds had been accounted for by weight. I knew I had given you and your men the correct amount of ammunition but I knew you would need them more than I.

The revelation began to have a profound effect on Berenger. A frown gradually creased its way into Berenger's forehead. Woolwich continued.

"The men, the South Australians charged straight-up into the ridge lines from where they landed. I realised they were in the wrong place, but I am only one person and I felt that I could give more assistance to them on the beach in the wrong place than following you to begin the assault at the right place. I'm sorry," he panted remorsefully.

"When I got to shore it was already getting light. I was hit in my shoulder several times by machine-gun fire, so I slumped into the bank to collect my breath."

Woolwich paused. His head nodded forward.

"Keep talking," Berenger said gently.

A pained expression followed; Berenger knew Woolwich had lost a lot of blood. The injury was not one that would have been fatal had he stayed on the beach and waited for treatment by the medic but he had chosen to continue, further risking his life in doing so.

"I saw you collect our men and the Queenslanders and make for the proper departure point on the beach. I knew you were right. We could see you from our pinnace but subsequent waves of them reinforced our mistake. I wanted to go with you. You have always demonstrated the most professional way to go about things but… " he nodded off again.

"Wake up, Woolwich," Berenger said abruptly.

"Sergeant Berenger, you are the best soldier I have ever met in my 20 years in the army. Your reasoned answers to military problems have always astounded me. You have always shown the greatest attention to the minutest detail. But sergeant, you have no empathy," he continued hesitatingly.

"Empathy will get you killed," Berenger thought but did not say.

"You have no empathy for the men because you have always been a soldier. You see professionalism in soldiering as an end in itself. The men idolise you, but you will only succeed in making any of them, who survive into a replication of yourself. Almost all of these men are inexperienced volunteers, who have civilian lives to return to. I have never seen you falter. You seem impervious to your own suffering. But to suffer is human. If you lack empathy, you lack humanity. It is not weak to empathise with the soldiers. It is humane."

"I need to treat your wound, Staff-Sergeant. Keep your hand there," Berenger said somewhat hesitatingly.

He went to the bucket of water and tipped a little on his hands cleaning them as best he could. When he returned to treat Woolwich's wound, Berenger found Woolwich had died.

A deep sense of anguish washed over Berenger. This was a failure. Berenger felt he could have saved him. He should have saved him. He moved Woolwich's body to one side. Woolwich was right. William's cold rationality had conflicted with the empathy some of the other sergeants had shown to their men in training. Empathy Berenger considered had caused men to drown disembarking over the sides of their pinnaces.

The idea that if he had no empathy, he had no humanity caused Berenger much concern. Disconcertingly, Tolga the sadist and Berenger shared a common characteristic.

Sergeant Berenger placed Woolwich's hands gently across his chest; shooing away an interested rat in the process. Wiremu assisted and quietly chanted over Woolwich in Māori. The ramifications of Woolwich's censure before he died began to sink-in very deeply indeed.

Berenger gently removed Woolwich's boots, tied the laces together and put them to one side. He carried no other items on his uniform. The guards had removed everything.

"*Kua haere atu ia ki ona tipuna* (He has gone to his ancestors)," whispered Wiremu.

Chapter 9
Doubt

"Whoever destroys a single life is as guilty as though he had destroyed the entire world and whoever rescues a single life earns as much merit as though he had rescued the entire world."

The Talmud

Avraham had travelled widely. He was well read. Years ago, in Constantinople, he had met with a kindly old bookseller called Mehmet in the Grand Bazaar. Whilst sitting on cushions around a low table, Avraham and Mehmet talked together.

Avraham thought it was unjust that he had to pay a tax merely because he was a Jew. "You are not required to serve in the Ottoman Army like the Muslims," said Mehmet.

"Oy," said Avraham, raising his hand dismissing the concession.

"Sometimes Elohim is unjust. I do not understand Him."

"The word, Elohim is a plural," smiled Mehmet.

"There is only one God," Avraham pointed an accusing finger at Mehmet.

Mehmet carefully poured them both another small cup of Turkish coffee.

"In the beginning Elohim, created the heavens and the earth," Avraham pronounced authoritatively.

"Oh," said Mehmet, in such a way that Avraham sensed his own uncertainty.

"Do you believe in an eternal Creator?" Avraham enquired.

Mehmet frowned for a long while saying nothing. The smell of rich spices drifted by, following a merchant carrying a bolt of delicately patterned Turkish cloth. Street urchins observing books too closely ducked away when they made eye contact with surly little Tolga. Tolga sitting on a rug behind them, waited in anticipation.

Finally, Mehmet took his focus from the Turkish coffee pot.

"Yes…" he said. "…and no."

Avraham dismayed, said, "Of course, there is a Creator and He is Eternal. How can the universe come from nothing without being created?"

Avraham had now raised both hands, scratching his head through his well-worn yarmulke.

"Do you think Schubert's music is beautiful?"

"Yes, Schubert's music is beautiful," Avraham looked quizzically at Mehmet.

"Do you think you can hear Schubert's music as well as a young man?"

"Well, I am getting quite old and a little deaf now. I think a young man would hear it a little better than I," conceded Avraham agreeably.

"But you would agree that a note played in Schubert's choral for Psalm 92 would exist even though you may not be able to hear it yourself?"

"Would you agree that it is possible the creator of the note in Schubert's choral could die of a heart attack and the note continues to exist in the absence of its creator?"

"If you believe in a Creator, how can you be sure His creation has not superseded Him?"

"Hmmm," said Avraham in a non-committal way.

"What then created the universe?" enquired Avraham.

"Nothing," shrugged Mehmet.

"Are you saying God is Nothing or Nothing is God?" asked Avraham critically.

Deep in thought, they both looked intently at the coffee pot in the centre of the low round table. After some contemplation, Avraham said, "I must go now."

Mehmet stood up, made a small bow. Both men wished each other well, Avraham paid for the least expensive Qur'an and left, leaving the Qur'an closed on an upper shelf of Mehmet's stall.

Avraham was left more uncertain about the relationship of Elohim with the universe after his discourse with Mehmet than before, but he exacted some pleasure from thinking about it.

"So many questions," he mused to himself: "…whether the Creator came into existence; whether His creation has been completed and whether His creation exists independently of His control."

"Oy," Avraham exclaimed to himself.

Avraham remembered Mehmet's discourse with fondness. He had seen Tolga bring in the prisoners to Maidos. The sight of Tolga brought the pleasant reminiscence of Mehmet but rumours following Tolga made Avraham gingerly cautious about dealing with him.

Avraham had other matters to concern him. He had heard through Jewish merchants delivering military stores by sea to Maidos that his contacts in Constantinople had discovered the German banks, which funded the Anatolian Railway Company had financially over-extended themselves; an egregious error in Avraham's opinion.

Moreover, there were engineering difficulties in forcing a railway track through the Taurus Mountains. Avraham considered if the German's were unable to complete the railway to Constantinople, German merchant ships would not be able to circumvent the Suez, currently held by the British in order to trade with the Middle East. An expression of grave concern came over Avraham's face.

A further rumour percolated in Avraham's mind. Some weeks ago, the Ottoman Army had commenced mass deportations of Christian Armenians. The Battle of Sarıkamış was lost by the Ottoman Empire in January 1915 at a heavy price of up to 90 000 Ottoman casualties. Blame had to lie somewhere.

To deflect it from himself, Enver Pasha blamed the Christian Armenians, some of whom had served with the Russians against him. Avraham reflected on previous recent Armenian massacres by the Turks.

The recent deportations would result slaughter, he thought pinching his chin between his thumb and forefinger.

In calculating whether to support the Ottoman Empire or clandestinely their enemies, Avraham considered his position as a Jew. Surely, the civilised Germans would not consider future massacres of Jews in such a way as the 'illiterate' Ottomans massacre the Armenians.

To Avraham, the Germans represented the rational and industrial West. The Germans represented the antithesis of what Avraham called the crystallised Byzantine beliefs of the uneducated Muslims. Beliefs, which enforced Avraham to pay a tax from which, the Muslim Ottomans were exempt.

Avraham was considering having one foot in each camp. However, he discovered from Jewish banking contacts in Rome, the Italians would join forces with the Triple Entente if the British attacked the Ottoman Empire. Avraham had worked out the Italian decision for them, before they Italians knew it for themselves. The Italians came in on the side of the British, the French and the Russians on 26 April 1915. Avraham quickly removed his foot from surreptitiously supporting the Triple Alliance.

As he lay in bed, in the quartermaster's store in the early hours of 27 April, Avraham shrewdly calculated if the Ottomans lost their empire, that he would move to the West – maybe Australia. He needed to make allies of the prisoners brought in by Tolga so that they might speak on his behalf at the war's end.

At first light, Avraham arose; poured some water from the pitcher that stood on his bedside table into a bowl and conducted his morning ablutions. Thinking of his meditations the previous evening, Avraham mentally drafted a plan. He would first go to the Maidos mess to collect rations for the prisoners. After Avraham dressed, he left the quartermaster's store and quickly skirted around the perimeter of the parade ground to the mess.

Recruits, who sat eating in one part of the mess, were joined by the officers of the most recent Turkish battalion to cross from Asia, sitting in another part of the mess. Some of the senior officers were smoking nervously. Avraham could see the stress on their faces as they discussed the disposition of their troops deploying to Ali Burnu. The mess was very busy. Avraham reported to a junior cook and requested the allocation of food for the Maidos gaol. He didn't know how many prisoners had been imprisoned, so he said twenty.

"Where's your requisition sheet from the quartermaster?" was the reply.

"I am the quartermaster!" Avraham snapped.

A box carrying fruit, olives and bread for twenty delivered to Arvaham, who struggled to take it from the back door of the Maidos mess.

Ali and Mohammad, who had just finished at the mess themselves and making their way to the Maidos gaol to relieve the guards, saw the old Jew struggling to carry the box. Taking the box between them, Avraham beckoned them to follow him back to the quartermaster's store.

Avraham asked Ali how many prisoners he had brought in last night.

"Seven," said Ali, standing with his heels together, arms at the side.

"I need you to select six cloth caps, six tunics, six shirts, six belts and six pairs of trousers in approximately the same size or slightly larger than the prisoners, that you brought in last night," Avraham spoke in Arabic.

As Mohammad and Ali diligently combed through all the sizes of clothes neatly stacked on the shelves behind Avraham's counter, Avraham collected a German uniform, which had been delivered to him for mending from his room.

"Where is Tolga?" Avraham asked.

"He's asleep," said Mohammad.

Mohammad did not disclose that Tolga had told them to wake him up for breakfast, but they intentionally refrained from doing so because they knew Tolga would get in trouble with his old friends, the Regimental Sergeant Major and the Training Officer.

"We have to relieve the guards so they can go to breakfast," said Ali.

Avraham pointed to the food and the clothes.

"We will take these supplies to the Maidos gaol. Come with me."

He unlocked the quartermaster's store.

Ali carrying the uniforms and Mohammad carrying the food followed Avraham, who skirted around the parade ground, past the main gates at the entrance to the camp and up to the metal gate at the top of the stairs of the Maidos gaol.

"Where have you been? You're late," growled the impatient guard.

"I have your replacement and the replacement for the guard at the bottom of the stairs."

"Good, I'm going," he unlocked the gate, ceremoniously placed the keys in Avraham's hand and marched off in the direction of the mess, leaving Avraham to lock the gate behind him.

Avraham directed Ali and Mohammad down the spiral staircase. Before turning the key in the lock, he furtively caste his eyes about the compound. The compound was amok with soldiers running about preparing to deploy to Ari Burnu. No one noticed anything different about the changing of the guard at the Maidos gaol. Avraham stole down the spiralling staircase. On the landing, he passed Ali and Mohammad and hurried them along. At the bottom of the staircase, Ali and Mohammad were reprimanded for being late by the Turkish soldier standing impatiently behind the metal gate at the entrance to the nave.

"I will report you for this," he said as Mohammad took him up the stairs to let him out.

"Leave the food here," Avraham pointed.

Ali placed his box next to the guard's office.

"Arrange the uniforms in six piles at the bottom, one complete set per man. Place the German uniform on the desk there."

Avraham took the keys from the wall.

"Point to the cage, which holds your prisoners."

Ali pointed to the second of the cages. There was no sound or movement from any cage. But the key in the lock of the metal gate at the bottom of the stairs had woken up both Berenger and Wiremu. Berenger watched carefully. He nodded to Wiremu, who silently woke up the remaining inmates.

Knives ready, Berenger made a motion with his hands. Unable to see Avraham's face in the silhouette against the candlelight from the office, Berenger prepared to kill him. When Avraham reached the metal gate, instead of saying, "Get to the back!" he said to Berenger, "Come here."

Speaking in English, Avraham said, "I have brought food and clothes, you will all quietly come with me. You will change into your uniforms. You will take your food and you will come with me."

The key slid into the lock and turned. Berenger slightly raised his hand palm open, and the men refrained from killing the old Jew – for the moment. They filed out in silence. Patrick Kearney, who had woken in the cell next to them, thought the worst.

He whispered, "Good luck, boys," as he thought the Australians and New Zealanders were being marched to their execution.

On approaching the guard's makeshift desk, Berenger spotted Ali, who had arranged the uniforms. Ali looked afraid. Berenger patted him lightly on the arm.

"Alles ist gut," he smiled.

The sigh of relief came to Ali's face. Avraham looked about the bottom of the stairwell as the men changed into their Turkish uniforms; he beckoned for Tom to get the attention of Berenger.

"Sergeant Berenger," Tom whispered.

Ali eyes opened wide.

Berenger? Maybe this was the relation of Dr Helmut, Ali thought.

Avraham directed Berenger's hand to the German uniform laid out neatly on the desk. This man appears to be the right size, Avraham thought, without realising that this man also spoke German. Berenger gave Ali his Australian army uniform with its South Australian insignia, to hide in a wooden box stored beneath the desk.

Avraham noticed the insignia and said, "South Australian," under his breath.

The connection between Berenger and Dr Helmut was confirmed for Ali.

Sergeant Berenger discerned the plan to escape but had not as yet discovered Avraham's reason. Mohammad returned without locking the gate at the bottom of the stairs, picked up the box of food and crept down the stairwell.

Avraham pointed at the box. The men filled their pockets. Berenger gently pushed Ali and Mohammad towards the box before he took supplies for himself.

He's making allies, thought Avraham.

Before they left the office, Berenger made them line up and inspected their uniforms. Ali and Mohammad, who were still unaware that they were complicit in an escape attempt, showed the men how to wear their uniform according to the regulations of the Ottoman Army.

Their boots were not Ottoman issue and they were dirty. Berenger intervened. Trousers would be worn bloused outside of boots. It was already light and if somebody noticed, Berenger would reprimand them in German. Before they left, they doused the lights so the remaining prisoners would not be able to see them in enemy disguise.

The remaining prisoners had indeed woken up. Fearing the worst, they wished the escapees well from their cells as they climbed the stairs.

"Chins up, lads," cheered the Lancashire Fusiliers.

"Good luck, boys," whispered Patrick Kearny from Munster.

At the landing Berenger stopped them.

Avraham said, "You will march out of the main gate. It will be open."

Sergeant Berenger added in English and German.

"We will form up in two files facing the gate. Ali you will be the marker, Mohammad you will be the left-hand guide. Tom, you will be last man in the marker's file. Wiremu, you will be last man in the left-hand file."

"You…," pointing to Avraham, "…will walk by yourself at the front-left of the section and explain to the guards, only if asked why we are leaving Fort Kilitbahir. Tell me what your answer will be if you are asked."

Sergeant Berenger instructed Ali to translate.

Avraham responded. "The soldiers are assigned to assist the stevedores in unloading a supply vessel that docked every morning."

At the top of the stairs, Mohammad opened the gate and the soldiers formed up in two files. It was about 100 yards to the gate. Just as they had formed up a Turkish Battalion were marching into Maidos camp to collect their new infantry company. Berenger saw the Commanding Officer standing on a dais at one side of the parade ground, with the remaining officers, Regimental Sergeant Major and some instructors in attendance for the graduating parade. One of the junior companies of recruits acted as markers and guides for the graduating company to merge with their new battalion.

Avraham gasped as Berenger barked out drill commands in German, attracting attention from nearby Turkish instructors, who stood to attention upon hearing them.

"March!" Berenger growled.

The section of Australians, New Zealanders, two Arabs accompanied by Jew, and a German-speaking South Australian, stepped off with the left foot in unison. The attention of the Ottoman troops returned to their own parade, which due to the urgency of the situation only required the battalion to march through the parade ground, the new infantry company to follow-on behind the adjutant to collect the new company's documentation. They would continue on their march to Ari Burnu.

The gates wide open, guarded by two Turkish recruits, one of whom Berenger could see was about to question him. Avraham was ready with his concocted a story; Berenger had thought to berate the guards in German to silence their impudence. As they approached the two guards, a plethora of Turkish expletives flowed from the mouth of Ali. The guards immediately stood to attention, heels together; unsure of the correct compliments to a German Non-Commissioned Officer, saluting Berenger, whilst the section marched through the gates to the port at Maidos.

"Alles ist gut," Berenger growled to the guards, who did not understand.

Sergeant Berenger, returning the salute, felt sighs of relief from the guards that they were not getting punished for some small infraction.

The bugle blast on the parade ground at Maidos camp signalled the end of the final parade for the company scheduled amalgamate with their new battalion early on account of the British assault at Cape Helles and Ari Burnu.

The bugle blast also woke up Tolga from a deep and uncomfortable slumber, where he had secreted himself into a spare bed in the instructors' barracks in breach of his new rank of private soldier. He was spotted, attempting to find breakfast, behind the mess by one of the Maidos gaolers. Had he woken up on time, he may have been able to slip into the mess incognito. However, on censoriously dictating to the tired gaoler that he had brought in seven prisoners, they both marched over to the entrance of the gaol to relieve the temporary guards. The gaoler was in no mood to return to the gaol with Tolga.

Upon finding no one in attendance at the top of the stairs, the guard went to the Regimental Sergeant Major's office to uplift the spare keys, at which time Tolga became very reluctant to accompany him. However, Tolga had already been spotted by the Regimental Sergeant Major, who had returned from the parade ground. As Tolga made an excuse to return to barracks to collect some item of uniform, he heard a familiar voice from across the parade ground.

"Tolga!" roared the Regimental Sergeant Major. A name that permeated the offices of the German Training Officer, the Adjutant and the Commanding Officer; and brought a cynical smile to the faces of the Turkish instructors at Maidos, who recalled Tolga from his previous unpleasant sojourn with them.

Tolga stood with his heels together with his back facing the Regimental Sergeant Major at the far end of the parade ground, completed a very unsteady about turn.

"Come here!"

Tolga began to march, in such a panic that he stepped forward with his right leg simultaneously swinging his right arm forward.

"Run!" roared the Regimental Sergeant Major. Tolga started running. He felt the instructors sniggering at him as he started to run across the parade ground.

"Not across my parade ground!"

Tolga attempted an about-turn at the double-march and fell over.

Chapter 10
Redemption

"Five days, about, had passed since we had entered the Dardanelles, vouched for by our experiences, the only true recorders of time's every varying flight. As one by one the five days had slipped by, the habit of thinking we were alone became so ingrained that realisation of the reverse brought very pleasant surprise."

Lieutenant-Commander Henry Stoker
Commander HMAS Submarine AE2

Fresh food supplies destined for Fort Kilitbahir arrived from Çanakkale upon a small converted troop-transporter, which regularly traversed the straights from Çanakkale to Maidos on to Gelibolu and back to Çanakkale. The regular supply-ship, which carried heavier cargo including carts and mules, arrived from Çanakkale once per week. Since mules and carts were in short supply at Fort Kilitbahir, Berenger marched his section to the port at Maidos, giving the impression that the soldiers would carry the supplies by hand.

Turkish troops from Asia assembled at Maidos port, destined for Fort Kilitbahir formed up in three ranks on the road leading from the harbour. When they saw a German Non-Commissioned Officer, the appearance of which, made them feel inferior and simultaneously resentful because he neither represented nor understood the Ottoman Empire, there were sneers and muted remarks, but no one suspected they were escapees.

Threading their way through the stevedores and merchants on the wharf, Berenger wondered what the Turks made of the escapees fair facial features, but observed that everyone was in too much of a rush to notice. If they did notice, Berenger surmised, they may have thought the Australians and New Zealanders, (Wiremu excepted), were Germans in Turkish uniforms. Had not the German sailors on the SMS *Goeben* donned the fez at port in Constantinople?

"Is this not why we have been inveigled in this European war?" grumbled a Turkish troop-transport's master, as Berenger's men marched past.

Avraham approached a troop-transporter converted into a supply-vessel, moored to the dock. Two Arab boatsmen were waiting for the stevedores, but the stevedores were overwhelmed with work unloading a larger vessel. The stevedore foreman, perspiration dripping from his forehead, was relieved to find that Avraham had brought his own unloading party with him and bid them to carry on.

Avraham spoke to the boatmen.

"We have orders to take these men to Gelibolu. You are going there to drop off supplies and then you will return to Çanakkale, is that correct?"

A lethargic "Yes" from the boatmen.

Despite the battles in Cape Helles, Ari Burnu and the present search for submarines by the Turkish Navy along the Straits, the Arabs affirmed their complete disinterest in Ottoman – European affairs.

Avraham sensing that sooner or later, Tolga would discover that his prisoners had escaped, said, "We will not unload the stores here as Fort Kilitbahir has sufficient supplies for today, but we will be required to off-load them at Gelibolu."

A shrug of Arab shoulders, and Berenger and his section embarked on the troop-transporter for Gelibolu; Wiremu grinning ear-to-ear.

***

Tolga, who had marched around the parade ground, approached the fuming Regimental Sergeant Major; entered his office and the door was quietly closed behind him. Shortly thereafter muffled threats and shouts emanated from the walls of the office to the sniggers of Turkish instructors within earshot. The German Training Officer was preparing for another disciplinary hearing with Tolga. The adjutant scoured his filing cabinet for a copy of Tolga's file, and the Commanding Officer slipped away from the parade for several minutes of relative tranquillity in private.

The Regimental Sergeant Major's office door was abruptly swung open. The Regimental Sergeant Major carrying a large metal ring of keys strode purposefully across the parade ground to the entrance of the gaol. Tolga hesitated and started to waddle around the perimeter of the parade ground, but the RSM reprimanded him with, "Follow me, Tolga!" in a deprecating manner of speaking that Tolga realised the RSM had not finished with him.

Reaching the locked gate at the entrance, the Regimental Sergeant Major called for the guards, but no answer. Turning the key in the metal lock, he dashed downstairs. Pausing at the landing, believing he may be entering an ambush, he sent Tolga down first.

Upon finding no guard to receive them at the bottom, the Regimental Sergeant Major waited for his eyes to adjust and carefully studied the prisoners in the dark. He said to Tolga, "Where are the ones, you brought in last night?"

Tolga pointed to the cell. They were unable to see clearly into the cell through the dim light. Taking one last look around for anything amiss, the Regimental Sergeant Major opened the gates.

"Tolga you check the cells. I will wait here at the gate."

There appeared to be nothing amiss amongst the makeshift desk and assorted boxes stacked neatly behind. Discarded Australian and New Zealand uniforms had been folded and secured in a box beneath the desk, which the Regimental Sergeant Major failed to check.

Tolga came back from the cells.

"They're gone," he whispered.

The Regimental Sergeant Major double-checked the cells with a perfunctory air, realising that he was being watched by remaining inmates.

"Check the infirmary," he whispered menacingly.

The Regimental Sergeant Major and Tolga walked the length of the nave, through foetid air and up a few short steps, across a stone platform into the infirmary. Several pairs of eyes gazed from their cots including the one pair, which belonged to Faber. From the Regimental Sergeant Major's concerned expression, Faber realised Berenger and his men had escaped. He rolled to face the wall, smiling to himself.

The Regimental Sergeant Major and Tolga having locked both sets of gates returned to the German Training Officer's quarters. He gave his preliminary report to the Commanding Officer, who had been given Tolga's file and was dismissed to send new guards to the gaol.

Tolga was made to stand to attention, whilst he gave his report. He was unable to explain the situation nor was he able to explain the absence of Mohammad and Ali. He could only speculate that they had been taken prisoner.

"Get outside and wait," said the German Training Officer, who began to quietly confer with the Commanding Officer.

"We will need to interrogate the prisoners for intelligence to be able to mount a successful counter-attack to dislodge the Australians from the peninsula. We cannot allow them to return to their positions to report on us."

The Commanding Offier agreed.

"Take a section of men with you. Take Tolga."

The German Training Officer frowned.

"Tolga is able to identify the soldiers if they have changed their uniforms. In my opinion, they have killed the Arabs, taken their uniforms and two of them are impersonating guards, for the other five," the Commanding Officer incorrectly surmised.

The Commanding Officer then looked at the portrait of Kaiser Wilhelm II hung behind his desk, and ostentatiously stroked his waxed moustache.

***

Waiting for the moon to set, the Submarine HMAS AE2 had slipped quietly into the Dardanelles in the early hours or 25 April at the time Berenger had descended from the *Scourge* into a pinnace destined for Gaba Tepe. The straits of the Dardanelles connected the Black Sea with the Sea of Mamara and the Aegean; a vital link for wheat exports out of Russian and Triple Entente imports to the Black Sea ports of Sebastopol and Odessa.

In August 1915 the German battle cruiser SMS *Goeben* and light cruiser SMS *Breslau* had audaciously berthed at Constantinople; having evaded the Royal Navy in the Mediterranean to the chagrin of the First Lord of the Admiralty Winston Churchill.

Shortly after the outbreak of war in July 1914, the First Lord had requisitioned two Turkish ships being completed in British shipyards: the *Sultan Osman* and the *Rashadieh*. The ships had been financed in the Ottoman Empire by public subscription.

The gift of the *Goeben* and *Breslau* to the Ottoman government encouraged Enver Pasha to side with the Triple Alliance. The popular Turkish disappointment with the British was somewhat ameliorated by German disingenuous benevolence. The German diplomatic coup was complete. Champagne glasses clinked as Ambassador Baron Hans von Wangeheim, held a discrete party in the German consulate in Constantinople.

***

The HMAS AE2, preserving her batteries, crept along the surface of the Straits, planning to dive upon reaching the mines laid at White Cliffs. Encountering difficult currents and winding course, Lieutenant Commander Henry Stoker realised he would be required to surface at the narrowest point.

When delivering his orders to his men, Stoker gravely announced, "Upon reaching Çanakkale, the narrowest point of the Straits, a sitting duck for Turkish spotlights and heavy guns on both the European and the Asian shores, susceptible to withering fire from Ottoman warships, alone in a minefield, amongst the Turkish Navy, we shall run amok."

Facing the prospect of imminent death, the Australian submariners let out a hearty cheer.

Carefully avoiding the searchlights at Eren Kőy bay inside the mouth of the straits, several times the searchlights of Whitecliffs passed over the men in the conning tower without reaction from the shore. Awash with adrenalin, Stoker pursued his lips and winked at his first lieutenant, who having regained his night-vision, responded with a silent grin.

Closing up on the European shore, Stoker prepared to descend from the conning tower as the AE2 approached the minefield. A Turkish gun opened-up on them from 'Swandere River'; one last breath of fresh sea air, and Stoker disappeared into his submarine.

Proceeding at a depth of about 75 feet, the submariners listened to the chains of the mines scratching and scraping against the metal hull; each time, experiencing the exhilarating feeling that they were cheating their own mortality. But each time the AE2 scraped a mine-chain and escaped their sense of exhilaration slightly diminished. When the AE2 became entangled, the submariners were momentarily satiated. When it became entangled a second time, some merely executed the ubiquitous cynical smile.

Passing beneath the guns of Kilitbahir, opposite to where the British submarine, the E15 had grounded on 17 April, the AE2 surfaced, periscope up, Stoker's face glued to the eyepiece. They were seen by Turks on both sides of the straights. A crescendo of fire from Turkish guns pierced the night.

Western Australian, Queensland, Tasmanian and South Australian infantry, fighting for their lives, were clinging precariously to the ridges at Ari Burnu.

At 6:01 am, in the moment of clarity, some men experience when faced with mortal adversity, ordered the AE2 to approach an enemy target: a Turkish supply-ship. In this moment, the submariners' movements; rehearsed and rehearsed, completely focused, until almost automatistic, guided their submarine towards the Turkish supply-ship beneath Fort Mecidiye until it presented itself within the cross-hairs of Stoker's periscope.

Just as the AE2 was about to fire, a small Turkish cruiser possibly carrying mines came into view. Stoker concentrated on this more suitable target. Within 400 yards, the range that a collision could prove fatal to both oncoming vessels, the AE2 fired a torpedo, and dove.

The explosion rocked the AE2, submariners determinedly steadying themselves there within. The sinking Turkish cruiser jeopardising the AE2 caused the submarine to traverse dangerously closer to the guns of Fort Mecidiye on the Asian shore. At 6:16 am on 25 April, at a depth of 10 feet, the AE2 became lodged within point blank range of the Turkish guns, conning tower exposed.

Some days later, the Arab boatmen guided their transport vessel along the coast in the direction of Gelibolu. Mohammad, having realised he and Ali had involved themselves in a conspiracy that would cost them their lives if they were caught, quietly discussed the ominous predicament with Ali.

Avraham explained to the Arab boatman their fate, should the Sunni's come to power at the end of the war, or should the Germans lose the war, in such a picturesque broken Arabic, that the boatmen began to caste worried glances at each other.

Sergeant Berenger considered his plans for getting from Gelibolu back to Ari Burnu. Simultaneously, familiarising himself with the coastal road and the various checkpoints along the way. He proposed to travel back down along the coast travelling parallel to the road and turn inland in a dogleg fashion rather than risk contacting unexpected troops in further inshore.

Wiremu had been instructed to divide the food into manageable meals, which would be taken with the soldiers upon their escape. Wiremu looked at Ali, Mohammad, Avraham and the two Arab boatmen, each of whom felt in turn very uneasy under his watchful gaze.

For Tom, the journey was exceedingly slow. He was kept busy with two of the other men, who had been instructed to divide rations into portable portions. The remaining four escapees, one New Zealander from Auckland and one from Australian from Queensland kept port and starboard watch. The two remaining South Australian privates were stood down and soundly went to sleep.

The Straits reverberated with merchant vessels caught in the wash of Turkish warships and minelayers. At about midday, the port and starboard watch were replaced and the remaining men ate in silence. Berenger had yet to determine why Arvaham allowed the vessel to travel further north into Turkish territory, rather than South towards the Aegean.

However, Arvaham knew that the vessel was expected at Gelibolu and that if it did not arrive, the German Training Officer would find out and realise the soldiers had escaped by sea. At this stage, Avraham expected the German Training Officer would consider that the escapees had made their escape by land in the direction of Ari Burnu.

Avraham's plan was to travel the circuit to Gelibolu and cross the Straits back to Çanakkale, where he intended to leave Mohammad and Ali. After refuelling, he intended to commission the Arabs to carry on down the Asian coast to Eren Kőy Bay, and recross the straits into the hands of the British.

Avraham intended to re-sell the food supplies at Çanakkale, (which he observed with concern, was being depleted by his fellow travellers). He had had the presence of mind to take with him the contents of the cash box from the quartermaster's store at Fort Kilitbahir, which quietly jingled in the deep pockets of his kaftan. This gave him an excited feeling of impropriety as he thought he heard his precious coins rubbing together when he moved around the vessel amongst the soldiers. But in reality, the sound was in Avraham's mind, the titillating feeling and his mischievous giggle ceased when he set eyes on Wiremu.

Avraham had predicated his eventual refuge in Australia upon the men, from whom he wished to take credit for rescuing from Ottoman captivity. It was hardly if he was in the Ottoman Army. He wasn't even in Turkish uniform, he thought to himself. All he had to do was makes friends with Berenger. There was one minor problem: Berenger did not like him.

Sergeant Berenger handed-over command to Wiremu and said he was going to get some sleep. He advised Wiremu that Tom should be made acting second-in-command whilst Wiremu was left to command the section. Berenger surmised incorrectly, but with an intention not to cause embarrassment, that Wiremu was unable to tell the time from Berenger's pocket-watch, so he instructed Tom to change the port and starboard sentry every 90 minutes.

In the Fort Kilitbahir dungeon, Woolwich's revelation to Berenger about his lack of empathy was beginning to reap rewards. Wiremu's leadership had not been undermined. He was unofficially promoted by Berenger. Tom, who was now section second-in-command, became responsible for drafting and keeping all section sentry rosters, the constant work would keep his bellicose personality in check.

A strange feeling of contentment came over Berenger, who hitherto would not have approached a simple problem in such a delicate manner. He fell asleep in the sun before his head rested against a sack of grain propped-up between two crates of olives. Strange dreams floated in-and-out of his mind. His dreams brought him back in time to South Africa. He returned to the converted stable where Breaker and the patrol had congratulated him for delivering a prescient weather report. The troopers were shaking his hand and patting him on the back.

Breaker mouthed, "Well done, William."

William heard no words in his dream but caught a reflection of himself in the barrack's window beaming with pride, eyes misted over.

Then he was back in Camp K_ with Cornelia. Her beautiful Delft-blue broken in shards on the ground. However, this time instead of leaving Cornelia whilst she wept for her broken china, William knelt down with her and helped her collect the pieces. He gently patted her on the arm and said everything would be alright, although no sound came out of his mouth. He tucked in Cornelia's children, demonstrating by action to Cornelia that the children were more important than the china. Cornelia wiped her eyes resignedly, and William left the tent.

The vision left and returned. This time Cornelia lay dead on her cot; and Juliana grief-stricken lay across her mother and deceased sisters, Geertje and Magdalena. Berenger picked up the emaciated body of Peter-Lambertus and gently laid his body on his cot. Placing the dead child's feet together, William placed the lifeless hands across his chest, closed his eyes, and carefully covered him with his blanket.

Juliana, who had stopped crying, but remained lying across her mother and siblings, watched William intently. He took one of the chairs in the tent and quietly talked about South Australia with Juliana: how vast and wonderful were the wide open spaces and rolling hills. He talked about the eucalyptus trees, the age of the rocks and the waves crashing on the shore. William told Juliana about his home in Blumberg and how he would like to show her the creatures called wallabies, who silhouetted themselves on the horizon as the sun set into the sea. Juliana stopped weeping and continued to listen intently.

Then a face appeared whom William did not like: de Wet. De Wet was shaking him, his face contorted. Mouthing something but no words came out of de Wet's mouth. Then it was gone. William was being shaken awake by Avraham whose bony fingers clasped him by the shoulders.

"The engine," said Avraham aggrieved.

The troop-transporter was about a mile from Gelibolu: the engine spluttered and then stopped.

The Arabs, less nonplussed than William would have expected, scratched their chins. Avraham put a hand in a pocket and nervously rubbed a coin between his thumb and forefinger. All eyes eventually rested upon William, who now awake, considered the situation. There did not appear to be a current, judging from a point in the landscape on the European coast, William detected they were very slowly drifting back towards Maidos.

One of the Arab boatmen, asking if they could draw the attention of any passing vessels to tow them to Gelibolu was silenced with "No!" before he could finish his sentence.

William noticed the sun low on the horizon. Within a few hours it would be 28 April. He could hear artillery fire in the distance from the south. He decided the Australians had not yet reached the Narrows.

After sunset they appeared to be no closer to Gelibolu, or Maidos; nor had they moved closer to the shores of either Asia or Europe.

"I need complete silence this evening," William whispered, as Ali took over port watch, and gawped vacantly at the Asian shore. A periscope surfaced aft of the troop ship and slowly gliding forward, parallel to the surface vessel began to cast its eye port. Ali, who had never seen a periscope previously nor was he able to comprehend a submarine, pointed to this mysterious pipe with a glass eye passing starboard.

The AE2 had not been the only submarine prowling the Straits in April 1915. HM Submarine E14 had slipped into the Dardanelles unseen on the evening of 27 April. Upon espying through the periscope's eyepiece, Ali's gormless expression on port-watch, Lieutenant Commander Edward Boyle, immediately taken aback cried out, "What the devil? Dive, dive, dive."

"Grab it, quickly," Tom ordered Ali.

I'll hang on to you. Ali grabbed the periscope, which slowly continued past their vessel gradually sinking into the water as it did so. Ali began to get further and further away from their vessel until his whole body was wrapped around the periscope and Tom, by the tips of his fingers hung on to Ali and to the gunwales of the troop-ship; all hands grabbing onto Tom.

The E14 quietly tried to slip beneath the waves; Ali refusing to relinquish the periscope, wailing at the top of his lungs, his enormous frightened eye staring down at Boyle through the telescope. The agitated submarine commander, breaking his characteristic public-school sang-froid exclaimed, "Dammit man, let go!"

Chapter 11
Intention

"Ko te manu e kai ana i te miro nona te ngahere – ko te manu e kai ana i te matauranga nona te ao."

The forest belongs to the bird, who eats the miro berry. The world belongs to the bird, who eats of knowledge.

Whakatauki: Māori proverb

Private Wiremu Tamihana, 3rd Auckland Infantry Regiment, had dark hair, brown tanned skin and brown eyes. To the European soldiers, he looked like a healthy antipodean Adonis in the manner, in which the British officer-class imagined them to be: sanguine, strong and unsophisticated.

The romantic characterisation of Wiremu Tamihana was only two third's correct. Part Māori, part Pākeha, (European) by the time Wiremu joined the army in 1914, he could speak Māori and English; read rudimentary Latin and Greek; had read the Bible, and had studied Darwinism by observation; all whilst working as a stevedore at the Ports of Auckland.

Wiremu was far from unsophisticated. To the white New Zealand recruiting sergeant, who enlisted Wiremu Tamihana and discretely entered his name as William Thompson, Wiremu was Māori.

Wiremu was by far the most apt recruit in the Auckland Infantry Regiment in 1914; appearing at the Ellerslie Race Course recruiting office out of nowhere with perfect white teeth. He had no criminal record. That is not to say Wiremu had never committed a crime; but to say that he had never been convicted of one. His happy-go-lucky aspect concealed a humble spirit, deep familial loyalty and a faculty for profound consideration.

When Wiremu was born, he lived on the marae with his Tainui hapu (sub-tribe) and whanau (extended family) on the Waikato River. In the evenings, Wiremu would lay awake in the

103

wharenui (meeting house) listening to his elders speak of the stories of his ancestors. In the beginning, there was Te Kore (The Nothingness). Te Po (The Night) emerged from Te Kore. Wiremu spent many years reflecting on the difference between Te Kore and Te Po, as he grew to adolescence.

Wiremu could ride a horse, swim confidently in the Waikato River and run faster along its grassy banks than his cousins. Both, Wiremu's father, Te Rau and Pākeha mother, Catherine had died. Officially, he was raised by his kuia; his grandmother, on his father's side.

Unofficially, Wiremu was raised with his cousins in his extended family in the ways, protocols and language of the marae. He had, however, been introduced to: English, God and the cane at the Wesleyan school he attended during the day. In the little church Wiremu attended on Sundays, he was introduced to the notion of sin.

Every Sunday, Wiremu, his kuia, his aunties, his cousins and some but not all of the men from his marae would walk past the grave of his mother in the little churchyard and attend Christian service. In the morning, the congregation was persuaded by the parson that God could speak English; and God's Edwardian, crystallised morality was more than coincidentally English. By the afternoon, on the marae, in the minds of the congregation, God could speak Māori. By the evening, the notions of sin, prudishness and the distinction of class from arcane, foreign and unusual table manners had disappeared. God's morality and table manners had become unmistakenly Māori.

Through the years, the well-meaning parson had unwittingly created in the minds of his Māori congregation a totally separate, totally heretical incarnation of God; the veneration of whom, would wax and wane with the success of the kumara crops.

Late one evening, when Wiremu was about 18, on returning from eeling, through the window of the smoking room, he chanced upon the proprietor of the Crown Hotel; his hands around the throat of his young mistress. Upon closer investigation, from the empty main street, Wiremu peered from the dark into the dimly lit smoking-room at the purple-faced proprietor, standing between the well-worn billiards table and the heavily inlaid Victorian door. The proprietor shouted, cursed

104

and accused this hapless young woman, now on her knees, tears streaming down her face, of larceny.

"Where are my gold coins? You are nothing but a damned thief!" the proprietor shouted, expectorating spittle.

"I swear sir, I didn't," pleaded the young woman.

Her protestation was met with a sound slap across her face causing her nose to bleed, and the young woman protested her innocence ever more vehemently. Wiremu thought the young woman to be barely older than himself, constrained around her waist in her corset, and around the throat by the proprietor. Her clothes did not appear to be her own and despite fully covering her body, were worn in such a suggestive way as to leave Wiremu in no doubt as to the doubtfulness of her profession.

Nevertheless, if not a lady, she was a human being and from Wiremu's perspective did not deserve the thrashing that she was receiving. There appeared to be only a few people about. A drunken patron shuffled out of the Crown Hotel and staggered off into the darkness; oblivious to the violence there within. Wiremu secreted his kete (flax bag) of slimy eels behind a large decorative container, from which grew a bushy verdant fern; together with its partner, framing the Hotel's entrance. Upon entering the vestibule, Wiremu passed through the cloakroom and pushed open the door to the Hotel's smoking-room.

The proprietor had the young woman kneeling on the ground with one hand about her throat and the other hand rose with a glass tumbler, about to smash it down upon her skull. Sensing Wiremu's intrusion, the proprietor's face, became redder and angrier, and he threw the tumbler at Wiremu. Wiremu's grin did not disappear, neither did he move as the tumbler flew past his face and smashed into the wall, covered with garish imitation William Morris wallpaper. The rich reds, blues and greens turning into a translucent brown colour as the cheap whiskey dribbled down the wall onto the sticky wooden floor.

Wiremu reached around the back of his trousers, where he kept his patu, (club). Producing it, the patu began to weave back and forth in front of Wiremu's face as he approached the proprietor. The young woman was immediately thrown to the ground. She quickly scurried away on hands and stockinged knees and made for the door through which, Wiremu had presently entered.

The proprietor, enraged at this rude interruption, grabbed a billiards cue, sitting in the rack on the wall. Wielding the cue in both hands, he exclaimed, "How dare you trespass on my property. Get the hell out!" and swung the cue with all his might at Wiremu's head.

Wiremu deftly blocking the cue with his pounamu (greenstone) patu struck the proprietor above the eye, cracking his skull in the process.

The proprietor fell to the floor. Wiremu looked behind him to see the proprietor's mistress. Instead of expressing gratitude, her face screwed up and she screamed, "You've killed him. Murderer. You've killed him."

Alighting from the doorway, she sought out assistance from the public bar. Wiremu ran from the smoking-room, back through the vestibule and out of the Crown Hotel back to his marae.

In a careful explanation to his kuia, he apologised profusely, for leaving her kete containing kai (food) for the morrow at the entrance of the Hotel; adding as an aside that he may have killed the proprietor with his patu in consequence. Wiremu was taken by a gathering of aunties to discuss this event blow by blow in the wharekai (dining hall).

It was determined by the aunties that Wiremu was defending himself and he would not be convicted of murder at trial. It was determined by his kuia that Wiremu was defending himself and he would be convicted of murder at trial.

"We don't understand your reasoning," said a confused auntie.

"Wiremu has a solid defence."

A moment's pause: the kuia sighed. "Wiremu will be convicted of murder."

"Are you sure? Why? He has a defence."

The kuia placed a wrinkled hand on Wiremu's shoulder.

"Wiremu will be convicted because: Wiremu killed a white property owner, there is a white witness, there will be a white jury, Wiremu will be subject to white justice and Wiremu is not white."

The women murmured amongst themselves. The men had long since retired to the wharenui. Only a dog could be heard barking in the distance.

Collectively, it was determined by the women of the marae that Wiremu Takarangi would become Wiremu Tamihana. In order to evade the authorities, Wiremu would no longer belong to the Tainui iwi (tribe).

He would join the tribe of a hitherto enemy in Auckland and live as a member of the Ngāti Whatua; with the whanau of his kuia's sister. The pākeha investigators, who would follow the morning sun, would not suspect that Ngāti Whatua would take in a fugitive from an iwi, who supported the Kingitanga Movement: an iwi, in which warriors fought against each other in the Māori Land Wars. But the pākeha were yet to fully understand the sophisticated familial relationships of the Māori.

Before daylight, Wiremu had kissed his kuia and his aunties, taken his horse and left for Auckland. Wiremu could barely remember his father but the man, who killed Te Rau Takarangi, Wiremu would soon meet.

Auckland, in 1910, had a thriving port; bustling with people and supplies. Carts uplifting crates and barrels as stevedores sweated and cursed to off-load them from the ships and manhandle them to land transport. Men in tweed suits rubbed their hands as their produce was loaded on board the SS *Te Anau* on Queens Wharf.

Wiremu worked hard for his uncle as a stevedore and even saved some money to visit the Royal Oak Zoological Gardens several times during the course of 1911. One Saturday afternoon, Wiremu dressed in work boots, suspendered trousers, his white shirt, sleeves rolled-up, sat watching a solemn looking lion pacing back and forth in its cage. His sandwich, a fashionably modern way to eat meat between two slices of bread, started to curl in the warm Auckland summer weather, so he ate a little more quickly.

The lion watched Wiremu masticating his food. Born into captivity; mange and malnutrition appeared to summarise the totality of this creature's existence. It was incongruous, Wiremu thought, that this pathetic creature could be considered the king of the jungle when even the flies that buzzed around the lion's head exhibited a greater expression of freedom by buzzing off through the cage bars to pester another trapped exhibit at the Zoological Gardens.

Wiremu, who had been introduced to Darwinism by his mother thought about Darwinian anthropocentrism. He thought about Christian anthropocentrism, which he learnt from the village parson, his mother's father. Wiremu determined commonalities between Christianity and Darwinism. When viewed from the perspective of anthropocentrism, Wiremu concluded that Christianity and Darwinism were about the same.

He thought both Darwinism and Christianity were flawed in perceiving existence from an anthropocentric hierarchy. If Wiremu was trapped in the cage with the lion, and only the flies could get out, then the flies would think they were superior to Wiremu and the lion. The flies may conclude that relative smallness and adroitness in flight were characteristics relegating Wiremu and the lion inferior to them; as neither Wiremu nor the lion were small nor could they fly.

If Wiremu was physically incapable of preventing himself from becoming the lion's lunch, the flies would consider the lion to be superior to Wiremu. Fly evolution had determined Wiremu had not evolved to win the survival of the fittest with the lion. Either way, the theories appeared go comfort the flies and they buzzed off from the lion to annoy the giraffe. Wiremu finished his sandwich and walked all the way back to his new home in Orakei deep in contemplation.

Wiremu and his new whanau attended the Methodist Church in Pitt Street, despite there being an Anglican church nearer to his home. But Wiremu was yet to learn the petty doctrinal squabbles of inter-denominational Protestantism. Wiremu believed in God as a metaphor. God became Tangaroa, Māori god of the sea or Tumatauenga, Māori god of war, or Jesus without the theological anguish experienced by the doctors of the church attempting to separate the roles of the Trinity. For Wiremu, God could transform Himself into any incarnation He wanted to.

The notion that the only people, who would enter Heaven, would be those, who believed in God in the same incarnation as they did, did not move Wiremu in the slightest. Neither did its corollary: the condemnation of everybody else to Hell. Wiremu's understanding of an afterlife amounted to reuniting with his ancestors. On the sagely advice of the pākeha clergy, Wiremu was advised that if he persisted in this belief, for him after death, it would be decidedly hot.

Working as a stevedore, as well as loading and unloading cargo, Wiremu was also expected to check each ship's consignment, which docked at the Ports of Auckland; correctly account for each item, checking it off his shipping manifest as he went. Wiremu's uncle Thomas, who had taught himself to read, was especially interested in any new books, which were destined for the Auckland Public Library. These items were to be put aside, whilst Wiremu's uncle would inspect them in private.

Wiremu quickly worked out the private inspection of the Auckland Public Library's new acquisitions was in order for Thomas to read them first. When Wiremu put aside the Iliad in Greek for a period of more than one month for himself, before announcing to his uncle that the Iliad had arrived, the Head Librarian became disconcerted and penned a letter to the Harbour Master as to the whereabouts of his new acquisitions.

This started a train of bureaucratic decelerations, which allowed Wiremu and Thomas to digest the new acquisitions for such an extended period that it took the books less time to travel by sea from the other side of the world to Auckland than to travel less than a mile up Queen street to the Public Library when they had arrived in port.

Thomas had seen the value of the tools of the pākeha, which he imparted to Wiremu to exercise with caution. They were not tools to supplant the existing intellectual tools of the Māori but should be carefully considered and pragmatically employed. The blending of two cultural traditions began in the tutelage of his mother, Catherine. Catherine sat on the banks of the Waikato River with Wiremu and his cousins and sang waiata (songs) in English and Māori. Then Catherine would talk with them about the river.

The spirits of the ancestors mingled with the sacred waters as it flowed towards the sea. Only the taniwha, who delved in the deep pools, the dangerous currents or deep, dark caves, remained static. Catherine said you could never look at the same river twice. Wiremu and his cousins understood that the flax on the far side of the river was about the same distance away from one day to the next as they played on the bank; that the Pōhutukawa tree, which hung low over the river, would display brilliant red flowers in the summer, only to shed them thereafter. But they could expect the brilliant red display the following year and they were never disappointed: but the river was forever changing and the water passing before Wiremu and his cousins would never be the same from one moment to the next.

The spirits of the ancestors in the river would simultaneously travel with the river to the sea and yet remain to comfort Wiremu and his cousins as they played in the shallow pools near the marae. The spirits would mingle with the sea at the river mouth and the sun would cause the spirits to ascend into the sky. The spirits would descend again as rain or snow into the cycle of the river. As Wiremu grew older, he concluded that although he never looked at the same river twice, it was not the river that changed. The change was in Wiremu.

He could catch eels with his bare hands when previously, as a small boy, he was unable to. Wiremu realised there would be a time when he was very old, that he could no longer catch eels with his bare hands, and then it would soon be time for him to join the spirits of his ancestors in the river.

This gave Wiremu a contented feeling, which he often expressed with a wide grin. He had no fear of life or death as to Wiremu, life and death were two forms of existence: one impermanent, the other permanent. He was in no hurry to experience the permanent form, but when it came, Wiremu would face it courageously like his father had.

When Wiremu's father was killed, Catherine stricken with grief threw herself in the Waikato, so her spirit could be with Te Rau forever. Losing both parents in such close proximity caused Wiremu to become bitter for a while. But some nights whilst eeling, he could feel their presence and the bitterness gradually dissipated.

Thomas likened Wiremu to Wiremu's father, Te Rau. Thomas said that Te Rau was a great warrior and a great leader.

"Te Rau was as impetuous and he was courageous," Thomas remembered.

Te Rau's mother was Wiremu's kuia. Te Rau's spirit mixed with the waters of the Waikato when Te Rau died; and Catherine's spirit mixed with Te Rau.

As Thomas, Wiremu and Thomas' wife, Ripeka, sat around the dinner table in their little house in Orakei one evening,

Thomas recollected Te Rau's bravery. Ripeka filled two glasses of port from a decanter, which rested on a side-table beneath the window, and placed the glasses before the two men, who were engrossed in after-dinner conversation.

Te Rau's war party was sent to extract utu (retribution) for a Tainui raid. But the Tainui iwi caught wind of the approaching war party. Te Rau was caught in an ambush. He would not leave the bodies of his men, who were shot by enemy Māori and Pākeha, waiting for them before the morning mist arose. Many were killed disembarking from their waka. Te Rau fought on bravely despite running out of rounds for his musket. He cleaved the heads of his enemies both Māori and Pākeha alike, in the final counter-attack. Holding his musket by the barrel, taiaha fashion, Te Rau bearing many wounds finally succumbed to a round fired point blank, sending him to the underworld.

"Who did this?" Wiremu sat fists clenched at the table.

"Who killed my father? This must be avenged!"

In an avuncular manner, Thomas smiled at his nephew.

A moment's pause.

"That would be me," he said.

Chapter 12
Intuition

"For God so loved the world that He gave His only begotten Son, that whoever believes in Him should not perish, but have eternal life."

John 3:16

Casualty reports from 25 April flooded into battalion headquarters at Ari Burnu and flowed there from onto General Hamilton's flagship HMS *Queen Elizabeth*. Staff officer, Lieutenant Colonel de Wet was swamped with the names of men: killed in action, wounded in action and missing in action. De Wet co-ordinated the evacuation of the wounded to Lemnos. He had not slept for over 24 hours. His eyes red from lack of sleep, his temperament sour, de Wet could not comprehend the inefficiency of the 3rd Australian Infantry Brigade. "How could they not have taken their objectives?" he said to himself aloud.

De Wet's cramped cabin on the HMS *Queen Elizabeth* became awash with reports allocated into three overflowing trays on his desk; his porcelain phrenologist's skull, the only remaining relic from his service in South Africa, stared blankly at him. Shaking his head, he dramatically held the skull in both hands, caressing its temporal lobes with his thumbs. The fading sunlight piercing his little porthole, de Wet was incapable of fathoming why such a backwards race such as the Turks was holding their ground.

The cabin door opened. De Wet quickly replaced the skull on his desk, squinting at the intruder now standing before him. Ascertaining, that this messenger had not caught him fantasising about amateur theatrics; he said, gruffly, "What?"

"Casualty reports from the 10th South Australian battalion," the voice said.

"Put them there," de Wet pointed to a stack of reports that had not been divided into: Killed-in-Action, Wounded-in-Action or Missing-in-Action. "Advise General Hamilton that the total number of casualties from the 3rd Brigade will be prepared before his next meeting." The junior officer, saluted, about-turned and left.

The lists of the wounded out-numbered both the lists of killed and the missing combined. This was becoming irksome to de Wet because the pages of his wounded tray were slipping off onto the floor. De Wet casually picked up a casualty report stamped in red: Missing-In-Action.

"Ah good," he said out loud to himself.

De Wet stood up to close the portal window through which, the gentle sea breeze had disturbed the arrangement of his reports.

Upon securing the portal, a name from the past appeared on the report before him, which caused him great consternation. De Wet began to feel dizzy. The name on the report said, 'William Berenger, Missing In Action'. A name that could ruin de Wet's career if the owner of the name were to divulge an account of de Wet's bizarre behaviour in Camp K_ during the South African War.

De Wet steadied himself and then sat down. There were only two people alive, who knew this secret: his delirium and his fugues, which he constantly kept concealed. One was de Wet and the other was Berenger. De Wet became concerned that the document only reported that Berenger was Missing-in-Action. De Wet wanted certainty. The only way that de Wet would be absolutely certain that the two men would keep this secret was that one of them would be dead.

***

The converted troop-transport drifted throughout the night on the Straits. Tom had not let go of Ali, but Ali had let go of the periscope; and the submarine had disappeared into the straits.

"Sergeant Berenger, look," Ali said as he pointed to the light of a guard-hut along the coastal road from Gelibolu to Maidos.

Berenger took bearings from the moon and calculated that they would be required to cover at least 26 miles as the crow flies to reach their lines at Ari Burnu. In reality they would cover more than 50 miles.

The men were by now well fed and those, who were not on watch had gone to sleep. Tom had pierced opened all the crates. He had discovered more uniforms, socks, boots and equipment. But the Arabs had not been trusted to transport weapons and ammunition. Berenger's men complemented their uniforms with equipment they personalised for their intended journey. Some put on an extra pair of socks to cushion their feet. Some cut the excess from their waist-belts to decrease weight: a few ounces here and a few ounces there.

There were two rifles, one belonging to Mohammad and one belonging to Ali, which Berenger had confiscated and given Mohammad's Mauser to Wiremu. There were only 20 rounds per weapon, but Berenger had no intention of becoming involved in any protracted firefight with the Turks. Berenger, Wiremu and Tom planned to evade the Turks whilst slipping back to Ari Burnu.

Their first problem was Avraham. Berenger had come to believe that Avraham wanted something for rescuing them so Berenger enticed him with the remainder of the supplies of the troop-transport. Berenger advised Avraham, with the assistance of Mohammad as interpreter that he would be able to re-sell the supplies back to the Turkish army when he reached Çanakkale. He thanked Avraham for his assistance but told him that they were not coming with him and Avraham was not coming with them.

Sergeant Berenger explained that the men were deeply grateful for his assistance. However, he gave Avraham his word that he would speak on his behalf if he survived the war and wanted to migrate to Australia. Berenger refrained from telling him that he did not like Avraham's calculating ways as this would have been to no advantage to either of them.

Sergeant Berenger could see that Avraham was disappointed but sensed that he appreciated their gratitude. Berenger complimented Avraham for his escape-plan from Fort Kilitbahir.

"Oy, away with you," Avraham said as he waved his hand and made himself busy rearranging the equipment in the crates; smiling in the crooked way that people, who are not used to smiling, smile.

Sergeant Berenger ordered Mohammad to stay with Avraham and the Arab boatmen. When the boatmen had fixed their engine, Berenger told Mohammad that he must return to his father. Mohammad did not want to leave his younger brother but, (having discussed this with Ali); Berenger advised Mohammad that Ibrahim would probably prefer to sacrifice one son rather than two.

Sergeant Berenger, Wiremu and Tom agreed that they should divide into two groups as two small parties of four would be less conspicuous than one party of eight. They decided that Tom would take the Australians; and Berenger would take Ali and two others: Wiremu and Harry Kuehn.

Tom's party would make for the high ground and travel parallel to a road along the centre of the peninsula. Berenger would take his party along the coastal route and turn inland closer to Maidos. Berenger advised his party that if they were unable to pass guard-huts blocking the road, an option for them would be to swim out in the sea and quietly breaststroke past it.

They split into their separate groups to discuss their plans. The ground would be undulating and difficult. They did not think they would be able to complete 26 miles during the dark hours of one night. If they reached a point near Maidos before sun-up, they would turn inland and hide during the hours of daylight.

The men carried one rifle per party and divided the ammunition equally. Berenger showed Tom how to fire the Turkish Mauser, whilst the rest of the men prepared their equipment. The Arab boatmen looked on dismayed. Berenger didn't trust them, so he hadn't told them where they were going. Instead, Berenger told Mohammad to tell the boatmen to stay with their troop-transport as he would be getting help for them.

Sergeant Berenger determined that the most dangerous part of the journey would be inland; even more dangerous when they reached the Turkish lines. Calculating that both sides had dug-in, Berenger's plan was to slip through or around Turkish entrenchments to reach the Australian trenches.

He knew it was likely there were Turkish search parties out for them. They were only able to carry food supplies for three days and water for two. Berenger doubted that there would be many streams to refill their water canteens and the probability of being caught by the Turks would be too high to attempt stealing water from them, so they agreed that they could remain for three days before their water situation became dire.

The troop-transport ran aground a few yards from the shore, at least a night's journey to Maidos. SBerenger shook Avraham's hand again and said "Good bye" to him. He shook the hands of the Arab boatmen and they seemed glad that Berenger was going to get help. He intentionally omitted to tell the boatmen that he had no such plan as he waved them goodbye.

Sergeant Berenger's party quietly entered the water and secured the beach before Tom's party waded ashore. Without speaking, merely a nod as the four men, two Queenslanders and two South Australians filed through and disappeared into the night on the other side of the road.

When they had gone, Berenger motioned for his men to stand up and move quietly along the beach in the direction of Maidos. He put Ali in front of him and Harry Kuhn immediately behind him; Wiremu protected the rear in front of the two remaining New Zealanders.

Sergeant Berenger took Harry Keuhn with him instead of giving him to Tom because he knew that Keuhn would be the most obstinate and difficult during their escape out any of the men in either party. Keuhn's effect as a 'morale-thief' had been devastating on his platoon in training at Lemnos. Berenger would never have imagined this snivelling little whiner would become an Australian Senator after the war, but in retrospect, Berenger was not surprised. He rated Tom's team as the strongest: two big Queenslanders, and two South Australian's from his platoon, whom Berenger had trained.

Sergeant Berenger's group crept quickly along the sandy beach in the dark. When the beach turned to stones and pebbles, they padded along the rough grass; all the while at a slow jog of about three miles per hour. After about two hours they approached a guard-hut on the road. There was a light inside the hut and they could see two guards. The guard-hut was situated at a T-junction and although they had not encountered any Turkish troops to date, the junction was busy with troops travelling inland from the coast.

Sergeant Berenger decided that they would quietly breaststroke out to sea at least 100 yards and pass the guard-hut in a wide arc. Berenger knew his rifle would get wet but this option was probably less risky that bluffing their way through.

Kuehn started to complain. He thought they should cross the road and pass the guard-hut on the landward side. Rather than tear strips off him, Berenger explained that they would encounter the inland road, which formed the T-junction. It was more likely that they would be spotted trying to cross this road than making their way around the guard-hut seaward side; and the guards were not looking out to sea.

Despite the time of year, the water was quite cold. They would have to jog for the rest of the night until sun-up or risk hypothermia. Ali, who decided to tell them he was unable to swim when he was chest height in the water, was towed by Wiremu. The swim was not so difficult as there was very little swell. They slowly swam their way in a large arc, not attracting any attention from the shore. The men landed some 100 yards further down from the check-point in a little alcove out of sight of the guard-hut; Ali stifling his coughs from inhaling salt water.

As they jogged along the beach Berenger could feel himself warming up. He made sure the men were eating and drinking as they went; conserving their energy as they struggled against hypothermia. Another two hours went by and they approached a rocky bluff projecting from the shore into the sea. They decided as they had not seen any Turks since the last guard-hut, this time they would risk the road.

Sergeant Berenger sent Ali up ahead, since he was officially in the Turkish army, and would be able to talk his way out if he was challenged. Berenger suspected if there were guards, they would think he was a simple half-wit lost from his unit and would send him on his way. Ali turned a corner and for a moment he was gone. Then Berenger heard him challenged by the guards of another guard-hut. He strained to hear but there was no reply, and Berenger prepared the remaining three to bolt back along the beach and cross the road. Then Berenger heard a string of Turkish expletives flowing out of Ali's mouth; and then nothing again.

Ali made his way back to us. "*Kommen Sie, bitte*," he said.

As they approached yet another guard-hut at a jog, the guards stood to attention and saluted as they jogged through. They stayed on the road for about another three miles until they came to the outskirts of a small village. It was dawn, and Berenger decided that they should seek cover for the day until the evening.

Berenger did not want to remain too close to the village lest domestic dogs come sniffing around so they crossed the road and looked for a convenient place to hide.

A dry creek-bed forming under a bridge opened up into a morning suntrap about 200 yards further up the dere. Berenger decided they should rest there. The warm sun was a welcome respite and Berenger congratulated the men on the quiet move during the night. Kuehn had eaten about half of his food and drank about half of his water. Berenger wanted to throttle him. However, Berenger calculated he would be able to make it back to Ari Burnu before the next morning, so he did not make comment.

Sergeant Berenger awoke at about 5:00 pm. It was still full daylight. He saw Kuehn wash down the last of his food with the last of his water; and decided this would not be the most opportune time to get into an argument with him. They decided to discuss their situation. Berenger calculated that it was unlikely that they would get any resupply of water or food between their present position and Ari Burnu.

The risk of moving from their position for at least 24 hours and possibly more without sufficient food or water would be a fatal one. They decided that they would wait until sundown and Berenger and Ali would cautiously make their way into town in search of food and water. Berenger took all the canteens but one. He poured the remaining water into one canteen and gave it to Wiremu to apportion until Berenger and Ali returned. Kuehn gave Berenger a surly look but knew that his lapse in discipline may have cost them their lives. Before Berenger and Ali slipped out of camp, Kuehn apologised.

Sergeant Berenger and Ali silently crept back to the bridge, tidied their uniforms as best they could and marched along the side of the road to the little village. A group of Turkish soldiers pushing a cart of supplies down the road asked them something, so Berenger abused them in German. Although he was unable to understand their Turkish reply, Berenger gathered they were accordingly abused, in Turkish. Ali's gawping expression turned into a wry smile. Berenger guessed he was right.

The Turkish village was a fishing village and by the looks of it, the people were very poor. A few mangy dogs roamed around the streets and each of the little huts had a pen of some sort, in which the fishermen would keep a sheep or a goat. Some village children came up to them in the twilight. They were interested in Berenger's rifle. Ali shooed them away, but they persisted.

As Berenger and Ali rounded the bend they could see the fishing boats pulled up to the shore. Berenger had calculated that they were coming close to Maidos and that eventually they would have to turn inland. One of the children pulled Berenger by the hand and took him and Ali to his humble abode nestled on the shores of Dardanelles. When his mother opened the door, she was taken aback by Ali but apprehensively allowed the strangers to enter.

Sergeant Berenger thought the Turkish soldiers must have been through the village many times and had probably helped themselves to the meagre supplies of fish. In any event, his first priority was to refill the water-canteens. The woman's husband, asleep by the fire, abruptly awoke and stood up. Ali spoke some broken Turkish to him, and Berenger signalled with his hands that they meant no harm to him or his wife.

A baby cried from under a swathe of rugs in a cradle near the fire. The little boy ran over to tend to his baby sister. One bed, one cradle, one table and two chairs amounted to almost all the worldly possessions of his family. Despite their abject poverty, Berenger became acutely aware of how the boy soothed his sister; and how the woman produced two bowls and filled them with some type of fish broth, which had been bubbling away in an iron pot suspended above the fire.

The stoicism of this little family struggling to survive impressed him. Their struggle to raise two children as their raison d'être was in itself, noble. As everyone in this little village was as poor as each other, Berenger concluded they were less covetous of each other's possessions as those in the middle-class South Australian environment, in which he had been raised. There were no books: they were illiterate. There were no pictures of family above the hearth: they were Muslim and therefore, iconoclasts. It appeared their sole spiritual consolation was their faith in Allah.

After some uncomfortable silence, the fisherman started talking with Ali. Berenger understood clearly one word that came from the fisherman's mouth: Tolga. Tolga had been to his home searching for the escapees. As the fisherman had not seen them, Tolga left. But not without taking the fisherman's daily catch. On the evening, that Tolga came, the family went hungry. Berenger thought carefully about this moving account: the plight of civilians in war was not one he felt he could realistically alleviate. However, in the matter of the plight of one particular family, maybe he could assist.

Sergeant Berenger did not doubt that Tolga would be back some day. Now that the fisherman had spoken with them, he could describe them to Tolga and if he did, it was more likely that Tolga would catch them before they made Ari Burnu. Berenger thought about Tolga's bestial predilections and it concerned him that the fisherman's wife would be home alone with her two children whilst her husband was at sea fishing.

Sergeant Berenger thought of an item he could give to the fisherman to give to his wife so she could protect herself against Tolga if he came again. It would require a giant leap of faith. Against his principles of rationality, an innate feeling that this was the right course of action arose. Berenger gave the fisherman his rifle.

Chapter 13
Transcendence

"And after you have suffered a little while, the God of all grace, who has called you to his eternal glory in Christ, will himself restore, confirm, strengthen, and establish you."

1 Peter 5:10

If Berenger entered into a firefight with the Turks on the eastern side of the peninsula, he was certain, his twenty rounds would soon be expended and they would all be killed. He ceremonially grabbed the fisherman's wrist and put his hand on the barrel of the rifle. Berenger placed the rounds on the table. He nodded and motioned to momentarily confused fisherman; and the rifle and the ammunition were his.

The fisherman looked at his wife and tears streamed down his face.

"Water," Berenger asked, cupping his hands in supplication.

The fisherman went outside and returned with a pail of fresh water. He went outside again whilst Ali filled up the water-canteens. When the fisherman returned, he had both arms full of dried fish: enough for an extra two days.

He told Ali, he had begun to hide his food because the Turkish soldiers would often come in and steal it. The fisherman still had enough for himself and his family. He thanked Berenger profusely for the rifle and ammunition, and Berenger patted his smiling son on the head, who was doing a little dance, trying to hold Berenger's hand.

When Berenger left the fisherman's hut, it was dark but the moon and stars were out and it was a clear night. This would make it easier to navigate but the concern was that they could be seen moving cross-country. Berenger determined they would keep to the dry creek-beds and any low ground as much as possible to keep them from silhouetting themselves on the ridges.

When Berenger and Ali returned to their camp, he redistributed the dried fish and the water-canteens. They headed up the creek-bed almost a mile until they started climbing up a re-entrant, which ended on a high crest, which they would have to cross to get to Ari Burnu. The cool air at the summit was a respite from the stifling atmosphere at the coast. The arbutus and scrub was about waist high and they crawled on their hands and knees near to the crest.

At the summit was a road leading down the spine of the peninsula. Berenger could hear Turkish voices on the other side of the road, so he lay very still in the long grass. He was unable to see from whence the voices emanated because they were over the other side of the crest of the ridge.

Sergeant Berenger heard an engine in the distance. A vehicle was coming towards him on the road; he was laying only yards from where it would pass. Instead of driving past, the vehicle stopped directly in front of him. Berenger heard a door open and close and another door open; then heard some footsteps on the gravel and finally some voices in German.

The Turkish voices from beyond the crest approached. There were a number of greetings in German and conversation was translated back into Turkish. The German officer was introduced as Herr General and the Turkish officers were told that he could not stay long. The Turkish officers were advised to make preparations for the incoming reinforcements for the assault that would take place on 19 May, on a few days hence. Herr General was making a preliminary inspection of the Turkish defensive lines travelling as far south as Achi Baba to speak in person to the commanding officer. He would return to inspect preparations tomorrow morning when it was light. Herr General expected the Turks to sap their trenches forward as close as they could get to the Australians, and then sap parallel to the Australian trenches, to reduce the distance that the Turkish infantry would have to charge in the final assault.

Sergeant Berenger immediately realised the importance of this intelligence. He remained still until the vehicle had driven away. Muffled Turkish insults followed Herr General as the continued to inspect the lines further down the peninsula. When the men had walked back over the crest of the hill, Berenger quickly made his way across the road. His heart sank to see that he may have stumbled onto a Regimental Headquarters. There were a number of buildings and barracks. Berenger could make out howitzers lined up on the parade ground, and most disappointing of all, he could hear dogs.

He ran back over the road and crept through the scrub to where Wiremu, Ali and Kuehn were waiting. Berenger moved from this position to a safer one further down the valley. The moon was high and they could see each other reasonably well in the ambient light. Berenger disclosed the information to Wiremu, Kuehn and the other New Zealanders as if any one of them made it back to their lines then at least one of us could tell the Australians.

"ANZACs," whispered Wiremu.

"What?"

"ANZACs: Australian and New Zealand Army Corps," Wiremu whispered.

The word that came to Berenger's mind was rarely used word of Germanic origin: bollocks. Berenger had never heard of the word 'ANZACs' whilst in training at Lemnos so he assumed it was 2nd Division 'bollocks' they had made up whilst they were playing soldiers on the pyramids together in Egypt. In any event, Berenger responded with, "ANZACs," to make him happy. Apparently from his grin, it did.

None of them were happy when Berenger said they would have to re-trace their steps between the steep cliffs back down the valley to move up next valley south of their position. This would take them most of the rest of the evening. Berenger heard Kuehn cursing under his breath behind him. By the time they reached a position where they could make their way up the next valley, they had almost returned to their point of departure. There was only about an hour of darkness left so Berenger instructed the men to look for a suitable place to rest for the evening. They were lucky not to be discovered but Berenger sensed there were more Turks in this valley and that the closer they got to Ari Burnu the more Turks they would encounter.

By about 10:00 am, Kuehn was snoring. Berenger refrained from the standard response of kicking him and shook him awake. Realising his noise, he turned over and slept on his stomach. Berenger was getting thirsty and they had only about half a canteen of water left each. Another 24 hours and all of their water would be gone. Berenger slept uneasily until dusk.

This evening he instructed the men to move slowly and deliberately, conserving energy as they wove their way through the arbutus. He warned them that just because they had to travel back down one valley to get into the next, there was no certainty that they would not have to do this again. Kuehn grumbled. Berenger looked at him and Kuehn became quiet.

"We travel in single file," Berenger said.

Despite Ali's obvious learning difficulty, he exhibited a dextrous ability to find a suitable route through difficult country. At their first drink break, Berenger told him this and he beamed. Berenger could see Kuehn was starting to drift off and knew he was already starting to feel dehydration through lack of fluid intake.

When they neared the crest, Berenger saw the road that traversed the spine of the peninsula. It was not quiet. Turkish soldiers were carrying large wooden beams, presumably to reinforce their trenches. Berenger saw an improvised guard-hut, which indicated to him that the junction of the road descending over the crest led to an important Turkish defensive position. A Turkish soldier approached the guards. A giant Turk emerged from the hut, his enormous bulk would have taken up almost the entire space therein. It was Tolga.

Sergeant Berenger did not know at the time, but the training officer from Fort Kilitbahir had gone down to the Turkish defences to tell the commander to be vigilant for deserter's crossing over from the Turkish lines. The Turkish commander gave the German Training Officer a quizzical look. Muffled Turkish insults followed after he left.

Sergeant Berenger estimated they were somewhere in the Sari Bair Range. They were close to the extreme flank of the ANZAC troops, currently held by the New Zealanders. Whilst Berenger calculated that this may be their last chance to find their way across to our lines, he heard a groan from Kuehn behind him. Berenger later learnt that Kuehn thought he had been bitten by something. His timing was impeccable.

Tolga's big ugly head turned towards the sound and he made his way to the road on the crest. It was too light for Berenger to move now as Tolga would see him and it was too dangerous for

Berenger to remain if he came any closer. Wiremu had seen Tolga approaching and slipped away with Kuehn and Ali back down the valley to their previous checkpoint.

Tolga cautiously shuffled across the road. Just as his giant foot was about to step on Berenger, Berenger sprang up. Evading his clumsy grasp, Berenger ran back down the valley. Tolga shouted for the guards. Berenger wound his way back down the rugged trail they had made on the way up. Listening to the guards' crash through the bushes, Berenger guessed he had less than 50 yards on them.

Shots went down into the valley. Berenger considered leading them on a wild goose chase rather than back to Wiremu. As he descended, the shots seemed further and further away and Berenger knew he was steadily making ground ahead of them. The two-hour journey up the valley had taken him less than 20 minutes to descend back to a previous checkpoint.

Wiremu and the others had only just made it in and were still panting. Without further discussion they left this checkpoint to descend back to the bottom of the valley again. Running single file in the starlight, whilst adrenaline was pumping through his veins gave Berenger an exquisite sense of vitality. He knew they had narrowly avoided capture. Berenger would speak to Kuehn about his discipline later, but their ability to maintain their footholds and run at such a pace for such a long period time made Berenger reflect on running in South Africa.

All the running Breaker had made him do on the veldt was paying off. Berenger allowed the slope to carry him down, bounding from rock to rock without consciously directing his mind to any particular step, only to the act of running.

Ali started to slow down at the bottom of the valley and jogged back to their starting point. When they arrived, Berenger felt the sense of elation in the men. They rested until they caught their breath and decided to head for the next valley south to search for a point to lay up for the day. Berenger decided that Tolga's guards had not followed us down the valley but that there would be extra patrols along the road at the crest when they approached the following evening. Berenger realised they had neither food nor water. He knew their entire decision-making processes would soon start to deteriorate, so he set the men to sleep and like Breaker would have done, he planned the patrol for the evening.

They would leave all but one water-canteen as all but Ali's water-canteen was empty. Berenger would fashion a garrotte out of the canteen straps if they had an opportunity to deal with any unsuspecting guards on the road. Wiremu had retained the homemade knife he had made in the Kilitbahir gaol. This was to prove very useful.

Sergeant Berenger was awoken at some time during the day by Wiremu, who told him to move out of the sun. Berenger complied by crawling further under a bush. His mouth felt dry and he knew he would suffer this evening. At least his stomach had shrunk and Berenger did not feel hungry, he consoled himself before drifting off back to sleep.

As the sun dipped beneath the hills, they stirred from their hide. Berenger had dreamt about South Africa. But they all knew this would probably be the last chance to make it back to their lines. Even from their position down in the valley they could see flares going up into the sky in the far distance. They could hear the pom-pom of Turkish artillery pounding into the Australian positions. Had it not been for the information Berenger had heard the previous evening and the urgency he needed to confer it to Australian headquarters at Ari Burnu, Berenger may have considered returning to the fisherman's hut.

Sergeant Berenger and his men slowly made their way up the third valley towards the sounds of the guns in the distance. Berenger was panting quite heavily after the first hour and at their first stop, they decided to move on in an even slower, more deliberate fashion. After two more hours, Berenger started to feel a little light-headed, and he ordered the men to rest for a while. Ali was lucid but exhausted. Kuehn, whose eyes were rolling in his head, had been short-roped to Wiremu using the garrotte, tied between Wiremu's belt at the rear and Kuehn's belt at the front. Wiremu was also very tired.

Sergeant Berenger gave Kuehn the last of Ali's water and he looked up the valley. The valley followed a long re-entrant, which inclined steeply at the end. If he had had any faith in God, now would have been an appropriate time to pray for the men. Berenger took a deep breath, and said to Ali, "Let's go."

Ali slowly got to his feet and moved off. Berenger helped Kuehn get up and Wiremu and Kuehn went next. Concentrating on his breathing, Berenger pushed on behind them. Mile after mile drifted past; the starlight barely making their path visible. Even Ali, hitherto sure-footed stumbled once or twice. As they ascended up into the hills, the vegetation grew sparser. Short bushes and knee-length grass supplanted the trees of the more verdant valley below. The air became slightly cooler. Berenger felt himself falling asleep and he tripped over a rock.

Coming to his senses he jogged a little to catch-up with the men, who had not noticed his fall. Berenger's mind began to drift again. He thought they were walking amongst a small herd of goats along the narrow trail. When one of them bleated, Berenger realised this was not a vision. The goats walked alongside them for a while. They were very nimble and chewed the long grass protruding from cracks in the rocks as they proceeded. The blisters on Berenger's heels burst and he felt blood and fluid running into his boots as he painfully made his way up the valley. Berenger was glad of the pain as he thought it kept his mind lucid.

One of the goats stood up and started walking on two feet next to Berenger. Berenger was too exhausted to think this was odd. The goat's body then transformed into a human being, but his ears, horns, beard and legs remained goat. Berenger thought he might ask him a question.

"Water?" Berenger panted.

The goat ignored him. Eventually, the goat turned to Berenger and said, "I'm Pan."

Pan wanted to know why Berenger hadn't been worshipping him lately. In their predicament, Berenger had a few pithy words for him, but he had the presence of mind to consider, what would be the point of speaking to a creature that wasn't real, especially since Berenger had never worshipped Pan.

Pan hypothetically opined that if Berenger worshipped him, he could inspire panic in the Turks, and they would fail in their attack on 19 May. Berenger decided to try to prove to himself that this thing was not real, and with some effort attempted to touch him as he delicately walked on cloven hooves. Berenger's hand passed through him and he disappeared.

Sergeant Berenger took another deep breath and moved on. The men were some way ahead of him now and he unsuccessfully attempted to close the gap by jogging up to them but the path was too steep, and he had no energy left.

Then an old lady came into his view just ahead of him. She was bent over struggling to hobble up the goat track just as they were. Her long dark dress was vaguely familiar. She wore a shawl and a dark bonnet. Berenger caught up with her.

"Water?" Berenger asked. She looked at him and smiled. "Keep going. You're nearly there," she said.

Berenger looked at her intently. "Don't you remember me, William?"

The voice was Cornelia's but she looked very, very old.

Sergeant Berenger was taken aback with surprise, they were walking along a narrow path beneath which, was a steep cliff. Berenger took a step back and felt the path give way. He was falling. Immediately, he realised this was the end. He had struggled enough. Berenger would fall to his death. But a strong nimble hand grabbed him by the wrist and yanked him back to the path.

"Keep going, you're doing well," the voice said.

This time Berenger looked at her and it was Cornelia again. This time as a young woman; strong and healthy; her voice was confident and sure.

Sergeant Berenger continued up the slope, trying not to look at her following close behind. He looked up again and there she was in front of him, only smaller and younger. The clothes were the same but this was not Cornelia. It was Juliana.

"Come on, you're too slow!"

Juliana took Berenger's hand.

She started talking to him about South Australia. About all the things Berenger had told her in South Africa. She told him about the wonderful sunsets; how the ocean crashed on the rocks, and about strange creatures called wallabies.

Sergeant Berenger felt a little stronger and with Juliana coaxing him along. He even managed to catch up with the other men. Juliana guided him over a narrow ledge, which doubled-back upon itself. They were nearing the plateau near the crest. The goats had appeared again and Juliana stopped to look

Berenger in the face. Berenger looked into her eyes. She smiled, saying Berenger had done well. He could rest now.

Juliana's face changed into Cornelia as an old woman and changed again into Cornelia as a young woman and again into Juliana as a girl. When Berenger looked into her eyes, she changed into all of them simultaneously, as if time had stood still. Berenger collapsed under a bush, desperately thirsty and slept until the late afternoon. He awoke to the bleating a nanny goat feeding her young.

Chapter 14
Actus Reus

"For thus the Lord, the God of Israel, says to me, take this cup of the wine of wrath from My hand and cause all the nations to whom I send you to drink it. They will drink and stagger and go mad because of the sword that I will send among them."

Jeremiah 25:15-16

Yungara was an aboriginal girl of 14 years. Her name meant 'wife'. When she was born, her father said her destiny was to become a wife. To her father, the word 'wife' meant a lot of things, but it could not be reasonably extrapolated to mean 'victim'. Yungara lived with her Kaurna family on the Adelaide Plains. Yungara could catch a goanna with her bare hands and she could and run like the wind.

It was when Yungara was running like the wind, one hot dry afternoon that she ran into the view of South Australian landholder Helmuth Kuehn. Kuehn, over-seeing work on a new fence on his estate, was looking for some female aboriginals to help his wife in domestic duties on their farm: especially young attractive ones. He rode up to Yungara on his horse. Yungara stopped and stared at Kuehn.

"You there. Where's your father?"

Yungara, who spoke only a little English, but understood Kuehn's words, pointed in the distance. In the distance, to Kuehn there was nothing but endless untamed plains as far as the eye could see.

"Go get him," Kuehn ordered the girl.

Kuehn turned his horse around and rode back along the fence to the farmhouse. After tethering his horse, Kuehn walked through the front door. It was another scorching summer. Dust coated and agitated him as he sat at the dinner table. A scurry from another room. A frail woman appeared. Older looking than her 30 years, she approached Kuehn carrying a decanter and glass. Without making eye contact with her husband, she poured him a whiskey, and slid it toward him, leaving the decanter within his reach.

"Dinner," said Kuehn gruffly.

The woman deftly padded out to the kitchen and returned with Kuehn's dinner and placed it on the table before him. Kuehn thought about praying but God had not blessed his estate with rain recently, so he decided God would have to miss out.

"Why aren't you eating?" Kuehn gave his wife a one-eyed glance.

"I'm not hungry, dear," was his wife's starved reply.

Mary Kuehn, a catholic had unconventionally married Helmuth Kuehn, a Lutheran. Six months later, Mary had a baby; but Mary's parents had already disowned her.

The marriage became loveless shortly after the birth of little Harry. Any affection Mary had towards Kuehn prior to her marriage, had long since evaporated due to two deficiencies in Kuehn's character: alcoholism and domestic violence. Kuehn would add paedophilia to his list of predilections before the month was out.

The next morning, Kuehn awoke with a hangover and a temper. There was a knock on the door.

"Get that will you?" Kuehn ordered Mary stentoriously.

Mary opened the door to find, Yungara, holding her father's hand.

"It's for you, dear," said Mary.

Kuehn, shirtless, shoe-less and hair dishevelled went to the door. Immediately, upon seeing Yungara and her father, Kuehn became obsequiously polite, covering his foul halitosis.

"How are you, my good man?" Kuehn then winked at the aboriginal man's daughter.

"Come with me, please."

Kuehn, Yungara and her father sat on the porch. Mary brought two cups of tea.

"You see all that land out there," Kuehn cast his hand in an ostentatious gesture.

"All that land out there, I carved out of nothing."

In fact, all that land out there, had been Kaurna land for thousands of years.

"I need someone to help Mary with domestic duties when I am working out there," Kuehn repeated the gesture of his hand.

The aboriginal man, who had neither been asked his name, nor proffered it, frowned. "I would like to employ your daughter," Kuehn said grandiosely.

"I can give her food and lodgings. You can be assured that she will be well looked-after."

After some minutes, the aboriginal man, who had too many daughters, and not enough sons, stood up; and without looking back, he left.

Kuehn took Yungara by the hand. She did not yet know the consequences of what had just occurred. Upon entering the barn, Kuehn said,

"Here are your new lodgings."

Then Kuehn took Yungara into the house and told Mary, "Assemble that old bed for the hired help, would you?"

Mary looked at Kuehn, and then looked at Yungara. A weary expression of sadness came over her face, which she attempted to hide with a weak smile. Kuehn took his horse and went off to the farthest reaches of his farm.

After assembling the bed in the barn, Mary inspected the barn door. She made an improvised wooden bar by locking a sturdy board between three pieces of wood: one piece of wood she nailed to the wall, the other two, she nailed to the door. Mary told Yungara to slide the long board between the two pieces of wood in order to lock the door every evening.

"To prevent predators from entering," she said awkwardly.

They then went about firing the copper for the washing.

When Mary was happy that Yungara was capable of plunging the dolly-stick into the washtub, she let Yungara carry on by herself. Mary looked about Kuehn's study, in search of any itinerant bottles of whiskey. After emptying a part-bottle outside so that only the slightest trickle remained therein, Mary set the bottle next to the decanter and went about preparing dinner.

At dusk, Kuehn returned, surly and parched from unceasing heat. Without brushing himself off, he entered through the front door. Yungara sensed an impending dread in Mary's behaviour.

"Drink," Kuehn ordered.

Mary poured the remaining drops of whiskey into the decanter and brought the decanter and a whiskey glass to her husband. Kuehn could not remember how much whiskey he drank the previous evening, but he became more caustic than usual.

"Dinner," he said.

Mary withdrew into the kitchen and presently placed a plate before him.

"What's this?" Kuehn said, pushing the plate to one side.

"Where's my whiskey?"

"There's none left."

Kuehn stood up and went outside. He saw Yungara slip into the barn, but that could wait until later. Hunting around behind the barn in a three-quarter wooden structure, Kuehn produced another bottle. Without waiting for Mary to pour the contents into the decanter, he removed the top and drinking from the bottle, walked back into the house.

Mary's face sank when Kuehn reappeared. Kuehn sat at the table, dinner untouched and proceeded to drink himself into a stupor. Mary saw Kuehn direct his gaze through the window to the barn.

"Let's go to bed, dear," she said, gently tugging at his arm.

"You go," Kuehn slurred.

Realising the ramifications of an argument, Mary retired to bed. She lay with the sheets pulled up to her chin listening to Kuehn stumbling around the house.

Then the moment Mary knew she would dread. The front door opened, and Kuehn went outside.

"Come to bed, dear," Mary called, but to no avail.

Mary heard whisperings from Kuehn at the barn door, but there was no answer. The murmurs became louder until they became shouts.

"Open this door, you little witch!"

There was kicking and banging at the door and then nothing. The front door to the house slammed, and Mary held her breath.

Kuehn left at first light. Mary told Yungara that she was ill today. She would be unable to get out of bed because she had stomach pains. Yungara entered Mary's bedroom and noticed Mary had been crying.

"I am ok. Just a little under the weather. I am going to give you instructions from bed today."

Kuehn came home just before dusk. He placed a full bottle of whiskey on the bedside table on his side of the bed. A sinister look from Kuehn was greeted with a weak smile.

"How are you, dear?" Mary was terrified.

Kuehn did not reply but went outside to the barn. Mary heard some hammering and banging and knew that Kuehn was dismantling the lock from the inside of the wooden door. Kuehn returned to the house.

"Yungara," he called sweetly.

"Has Mary shown you how to cook dinner?"

Yungara appeared from the kitchen carrying an inexperienced interpretation of Mary's dinner instructions.

"That looks lovely, Yungara. Why don't you sit down and eat with me?"

"Why don't you go into the bedroom and get the bottle on the table next to my bed?" Yungara got up to enter the room. Mary, who had been listening, reached over to grab the bottle before Yungara could remove it, but cramped up in pain as she did so. Yungara rushed out of the room, leaving Mary to deal with her internal bleeding.

Fever overcame Mary, as she lay in agony in bed. She was in immense pain. Mary heard the front door open and she heard Kuehn take Yungara out to the barn. The fever overcame her again and she drifted off into unconsciousness. Mary was awoken by screams from the barn. The screams momentarily brought her to her senses as she sat up. The screams became louder and Mary crawled out of bed in a fugue. On her hands and knees, blood trickling down her legs, Mary crawled to the wardrobe where Kuehn kept his loaded shotgun.

With the last of her energy, Mary crawled with the shotgun to a position on the floor in front of the front door. Mary heard the screams subside into sobs; and she passed out again. Suddenly, the front door flew open, swinging so hard against the wall that a picture of Kuehn, holding the shotgun, fell from the wall and smashed onto the floor. Mary awoke, and fired at the silhouette in the doorway. Kuehn fell down, dead.

In court number one, Adelaide Supreme Court, Justice Tandy presiding, Mary Kuehn was arraigned. To the charge of the murder of her husband Helmuth Kuehn, Mary entered a plea of Not Guilty. Gasps could be heard from the public gallery. The criminal case of the murderer wife had already been printed in the newspapers. How could she plead not guilty? Mary Kuehn had the loaded shotgun in her hands. She pointed it at her husband, poor Helmuth Kuehn. She intended to shoot him and she shot him. Intention or reckless intention as far as the newspapers were concerned, Mary Kuehn was guilty.

Yungara had run back to her family and could not be found. The prosecutor, Mr Reginald Robertson KC submitted that in this case, Mary Kuehn should not be able to rely on self-defence as a defence. Mary Kuehn was under no immediate threat from her husband. An alleged assault on a third party could not be taken into consideration as there was no evidence before the Court that an assault actually occurred. Therefore, Mary Kuehn could not rely on coming to the defence of another.

Mr Robertson KC advised the court that Mary Kuehn would allege her domestic servant was assaulted in the barn, but police would testify that Helmuth Kuehn's body was found in the doorway of his own home. It was irrational that Mary Kuehn could be allowed to rely on self-defence in this case. Either there was no assault in the barn or any alleged assault was historical and irrelevant. There was no evidence of any previous assault on Mary Kuehn from Helmuth Kuehn. She had never made any complaint to the police previously.

Her internal bleeding on the day in question was commonplace in a woman, who had recently given birth. So too was her hysterical condition; suffered by women, it was called post-partum depression. Justice Tandy raised an eyebrow, which Mr Robertson perspicaciously observed. Mr Robertson continued. Mary Kuehn's current allegations of domestic abuse could not reasonably be taken seriously. Justice Tandy agreed.

The male jury listened intently as the prosecutor opened the case for the Crown. Helmut Kuehn was an honest hard-working Lutheran, who married Mary O'Callaghan in a time of delicacy. Mr Kuehn has through his own hard work acquired and extended his land-holdings throughout his lifetime. He had proven himself to be a leader in the rural South Australian community.

Mary O'Callaghan brought nothing into her marriage with Helmuth Kuehn. There was no dowry and her parents had disowned her. When Helmuth Kuehn died, the farm, the homestead and all Mr Kuehn's holdings would belong to Mary

Kuehn neé O'Callaghan. Mr Robertson KC stood silently for a long time, looking at each jury member in the eye, as if the outcome of the war depended on it.

Justice Tandy invited Mr Berenger, barrister to commence submissions. "Mr Berenger, do you wish to make an opening statement for the defence?"

"Yes, your Honour. Mr Foreman, gentlemen of the jury. Mary Kuehn did not murder her husband Helmut Kuehn. In order to reach your verdict, the jury must be satisfied beyond reasonable doubt of two matters: that Mary Kuehn killed Helmuth Kuehn; and that Mary Kuehn intended to kill Helmut Kuehn or was reckless as to whether firing the shotgun at him would kill him."

"I ask the jury to consider intention in terms of consciousness and volition. A case where the body acts in the absence of the intention of the mind is called automatism. The case law relating to automatism, or physical acts or omissions, which are controlled by physical causes in the absence of consciousness, are divided into four discrete categories: the action was conscious and volitional. In this instance, Mary Kuehn would be conscious and intention was volitional. Mary Kuehn would have intended to kill Helmut Kuehn, and she would have killed Helmuth Kuehn. Mary Kuehn would be guilty of murder, but this is not the case you are required to decide.

The action was unconscious and involitional. In this instance, for example, Mary Kuehn is lying on the floor either asleep or unconscious, and her finger involuntarily twitches on the trigger of the shotgun thus killing Helmuth Kuehn. Mary Kuehn's action is both unconscious and involitional. She would be not guilty of murder. But Mary Kuehn will testify that she had just woken up. Mary Kuehn does not contest the allegation that she shot Helmuth Kuehn."

A gasp from the public gallery. Mr Berenger paused. "Mary Kuehn contests the allegation that she shot him consciously.

The third category is that the act conscious and involitional: for example, a reflex, perhaps an uncontrollable sneeze. In this case, Mary Kuehn would claim an involuntary physiological action caused her to pull the trigger of the shotgun. In this case, Mary Kuehn will be not guilty of murder, as the act was involitional, although she may be guilty of manslaughter. But Mary Kuehn is not charged with manslaughter, she is charged with murder. Mary Kuehn would be not guilty of murder because the act was involitional.

The final category is unconscious and volitional. In this instance, Mr Foreman and gentlemen of the jury, I ask you to consider, what is consciousness? Would the jury accept there are states of mind between when one is asleep or unconscious and when one is awake? By awake, I mean fully lucid, or lucid enough to make decisions from which, culpability could arise. Would the jury accept that a person could be under such extreme pain or fatigue, that the decisions a person makes may not be conscious decisions? Perhaps, soldiers serving in the present war may find themselves in a situation, where fatigue, physical injury or stress could invite actions or omissions, to which our legal concept of consciousness would fall below the standard of culpability."

Mr Berenger paused dramatically, "…would the jury accept, that a person may be suffering from an injury or an illness, not being an internal illness of the mind; that some decisions are not conscious decisions; or that some decisions are decisions, which would not attract culpability? Mr Foreman, gentlemen of the jury; if you could you accept that there are mental states between a fully conscious defendant and unconscious defendant; and you could accept that it would be reasonable to believe in this case that Mary Kuehn, suffering from a severe injury to the lower abdomen; one in which she bled profusely and could not walk but had to crawl across the floor, I put it to you that your verdict would be 'Not Guilty'."

A further dramatic pause: "Where Mary Kuehn, who will give evidence that she had either fallen asleep or passed out, upon being immediately awoken by a picture falling to the floor and smashing on the ground after the front door of her home was violently swung open and shot Helmuth Kuehn; would the jury accept Mary Kuehn's actions were actions below the level where conscious actions attract culpability? If the jury cannot, beyond reasonable doubt find Mary Kuehn culpable of murder, the appropriate verdict is Not Guilty."

The Court was adjourned and jury dismissed. His Honour advised the jury not to speak about the trial with their families at home or colleagues at work. But since the newspapers announced the Mary Kuehn murder trial as the leading headline,

His Honour realised that warning the jury not to subject themselves to external influences, would be akin to asking them not to think of a kangaroo.

Upon cross-examination of police by Mr Berenger, the jury learnt that: a bed had been set up in the barn. An empty whiskey bottle was found under the bed. There was blood on the sheets, and the blood belonged to neither Mary nor Helmuth Kuehn.

An eminent German psychiatrist, who had studied with Freud, gave evidence under examination from Mr Robertson KC that Mary Kuehn's recent rejection by her mother and father after they had discovered she was pregnant gave rise to displaced feelings of resentment against them, which Mary Kuehn may have acted out against her husband.

As the trial wore on, neither Mr Robertson KC nor Mr Berenger could ascertain the effect their arguments had on the jury. However, they could see that the evidence presented by them caused the jury to become more and more perturbed and that eventually they would be required to make a difficult decision. Every day the jury would retire wearier and more confused.

After closing submissions from counsel for the defence, Mr Berenger, His Honour summed up the case and directed questions for the jury to decide.

"If, as Mr Robertson has argued, Mr Berenger's argument is too Cartesian, and you find consciousness and voluntariness cannot separated in this case, you should return a guilty verdict. If you accept Mr Berenger's 'ghost in the machine' argument, that at the time, when Mary Kuehn shot her husband, she could not be said to be legally conscious, and the Crown had not proved their case beyond reasonable doubt, you should acquit."

The jury retired for three days. The public gallery was full to the brim. At least one newspaper already had the verdict of 'Justice is Served: Mary Kuehn Guilty' ready to be printed as its headline. The words, 'Shock Decision: Mary Kuehn found Not Guilty' was the alternative. Mary Kuehn fainted in the witness box when Mr Foreman announced the verdict as guilty.

Chapter 15
Sacrifice

"Ka mate, ka mate! ka ora! ka ora!
Ka mate! ka mate! ka ora! ka ora!
(It is death! It is death! It is life! It is life!)"

Te Rauparaha
1820

Wiremu had captured the nanny goat and Ali was presently milking it into the water-canteen. For the third time, they had made it to the plateau on top of the long ridgeline. About 500 yards to their front through the copse of scrubby arbutus and mountain grass Berenger heard Turkish machine-gun fire. To their rear, he could see the Straits of the Dardanelles. Through the haze in the distance, Berenger could discern Çanakkale Asia.

It was late in the afternoon and although on the shores of Ari Burnu it would have been sweltering, the mild breeze on the crest of the ridgeline refreshed their aching limbs. Ali gave the water-canteen to Kuehn first, as he had suffered the most and was hardly capable of moving. Ali drank next then gave the canteen to Wiremu. Responding with a grin, Wiremu merely had a sip, and attempted to pass the canteen to Berenger. Berenger pushed his hand back.

"Carry on, Wiremu. Keep drinking."

Out of the group, Berenger drank last. It was warm and sticky, and he could feel life re-energising his body. Berenger rested momentarily. Ali was chewing something. He looked at him closely and Ali offered Berenger a cicada. Berenger decided he was hungry, but he wasn't that hungry. He knew from the sound of machine-gun fire to their front, the Turkish trenches were less than 500 yards down the other side of the crest.

As the milk settled in his stomach, a thought came into Berenger's mind. He raised his head over the arbutus to look back down the valley. Berenger saw the road snaking away in both directions both north and south. They had crossed the road last night, without being detected by the Turks. Berenger hadn't even realised it.

"Praise, the Lord," he whispered absent-mindedly.

Wiremu heard him. "Praise the Lord," he said.

Sergeant Berenger frowned at him. Wiremu grinned back.

They were able to crawl forward to observe the Turkish entrenchments without being seen. It appeared they were still on the far left of the Ari Burnu position, as seen from the Aegean Sea. To their right front was the long curvature of Sulva Bay. Looking either side, along the ridgeline, it appeared they could be on the highest ground of the peninsula but Berenger decided not to look out above the vegetation for fear of being spotted.

The Turkish trench zigzagged to the left and right, parallel to the crest of the ridgeline and faced out over Ari Burnu. A sap trench extended forward at the head of which, two machine-gunners manned their machine-gun.

The as the sun dipped beneath the horizon, a sniper-party of two approached the Turkish machine gunners and slithered off towards the New Zealand trench system. Shortly afterwards, a party of two unarmed Turkish soldiers slithered over the top of the parapet into No Man's Land. To what purpose, Berenger was unable to immediately ascertain. Within a few minutes, the two unarmed soldiers re-appeared on hands and knees carrying an injured Turkish soldier between them.

They were a rescue party. Then an idea dawned on Berenger. They would all slip through the Turkish machine-gun emplacement as rescue parties. They would wait until one of the machine-gunners retired to get his replacement. This way there would be only one person manning the machine-gun and if he became suspicious of Berenger's German uniform, Berenger would garrotte him. On these grounds, Wiremu and Ali, who at least spoke some Turkish, would go first. Berenger suggested they should veer right as he thought that their left flank would be more heavily covered by machine-gun fire than their right. Then Kuehn and Berenger would slither right and crawl their way to the New Zealand trench system.

The possibility that they would be killed by New Zealand snipers was greater than the possibility that they would be killed by Turkish ones once they reached about the halfway point, which was only about 50 yards out of the Turkish trench. Berenger also considered that they may encounter New Zealand raiding parties, Turkish bombing parties, New Zealand parties attempting to snatch Turkish prisoners, Turkish snipers and both sides trying to conduct reconnaissance and surveillance: very busy No Man's Land indeed.

Eventually, one of the Turkish gunners left the machine-gun to get the replacement for the remaining gunner. Berenger calculated that they did not have long, perhaps a few minutes at most. If the gunner returned with a replacement, they would have three Turks to deal with. Wiremu and Ali slipped over the crest and into the Turkish trench. Kuehn and Berenger followed less than a minute behind.

Berenger heard Ali say, "Rescue party of four," in Turkish to the machine-gunner.

Good on you, mate, Berenger thought. Now he would not have to speak to the machine-gunner, who just grunted as Berenger lightly tapped him on the shoulder in the darkness announcing that Kuehn and he were about to slither over the top of the parapet.

As Berenger crawled into the dark, a New Zealand flare lit up the sky. *Bless you*, he thought. If the flare had gone up 30 seconds earlier, they would have been found out. A firefight between the Turkish snipers and the New Zealand infantry was taking place in the position that Wiremu and Ali were crawling towards.

"Kuehn, come here," Berenger whispered.

Kuehn slithered up to him. The ground was undulating but there was little cover and most of the vegetation had been shot away. Berenger could see the sandbags of the New Zealand infantry less than 50 yards to their front. Between them were one or two shell holes from rounds fired by the Royal Navy, currently stationed in the Aegean off the coast of Ari Burnu. Berenger saw several Turkish dead and many more New Zealand dead, strewn out and bloated on the ground. Some of them must have been there since 25 April.

"Kuehn, you stay right behind me," Berenger ordered.

"When we're 20 yards or so from the New Zealanders, I'll call to them that we're coming through. I hope they're a bit more discriminating than Tom or we'll both get shot."

Sergeant Berenger slithered forward using the dead bodies for cover and concealment. As they zigzagged closer to about 40 yards from the New Zealand trenches, one of the bodies groaned.

The body was Turkish. Berenger took his water canteen and slowly poured the remaining goat's milk into the dying man's mouth. Berenger placed his hand across this man's arm to comfort him. His tunic was covered in dried blood. Berenger whispered, "*Bismillah hir-Rahman nir-Rahim...* (In the name of God, most Gracious, most Compassionate...)." The Turk's groans subsided, and his breathing became relaxed. He was lying on his back looking directly up into the clear sky; the stars twinkling invitingly across the Aegean. Then he breathed no more.

A muzzle flash from the New Zealand trenches, and then many muzzle flashes. Bullets began whizzing around them. Bullets started whizzing from the Turkish trenches in response. Berenger looked behind him. The Turkish snipers in No Man's Land had been seen by the New Zealand sentries in their lines. The Turkish covering fire was to enable the snipers to scramble back to their trenches.

Then Berenger saw the silhouette of a figure stand up.

"Get down, you fool," Berenger whispered loudly, but to no avail.

It was Wiremu. They were only about 20 yards away from Berenger, and less than 40 yards from safety. They'd been crawling around for the best part of an hour oblivious to each other's proximity.

Wiremu grinned and said, "Go to your trenches. I am going to my ancestors. Go now, go!"

Wiremu stood with his legs wide apart, he raised his hands, slapped his thighs, looking to the sky father, Wiremu chanted, "Ka mate, ka mate, ka ora, ka ora..."

A voice came shouted from the New Zealand trench. "Hold your fire he's a kiwi!"

At that moment a volley of fire from the Turkish trench ripped into Wiremu's back. He stood momentarily and fell dead.

"Crawl, Kuehn, crawl!" slithering forward it was the longest 30 seconds of Berenger's life.

Berenger felt a Turkish round go through the bottom of his water-canteen and exit through the top, whizzing past his head.

Sergeant Berenger changed directions slithering further left; voices to his front.

"Crawl forward. Crawl forward. Not too far too your left. Come on, lads," came the cheers from between the sandbags.

Then a stream of expletives was heard from behind Berenger. Kuehn had been shot in the foot.

"Kuehn, hold on to me, man!" Berenger shouted.

Kuehn wrapped his arms around my leg, and Berenger crawled forward again. The crescendo of machine-gun fire opened up to his right within a body length. A long New Zealand arm reached over the parapet and dragged Berenger and Kuehn into their trench. Kuehn's Australian cursing and swearing became so severe Berenger was afraid the New Zealanders might throw him back over the top.

But they were marvellous. Not so marvellous to Ali however, whom I saw diving into the trench a few yards further down.

"Watch out, a Turk's got in the trench!" one of the New Zealanders caught him and another was about to strike him in the face-in with the butt of his rifle.

"Stop! He one of ours!" Berenger shouted indignantly: momentarily oblivious of the fact he was wearing a German uniform.

"Sergeant Mackintosh, 3rd Auckland Infantry Regiment," a voice whispered in the dark. "Sergeant Berenger, 10th South Australian," Berenger responded.

"Joe, take these men down to the medics," Mackintosh ordered one of his soldiers. "Who's that?" Mackintosh pointed to Ali, gawping, bewildered and being restrained by two burly New Zealanders.

"He's one of ours," Berenger said.

"Joe, take all three of them down to Company Headquarters. I will make a report once I've tidied things up here a bit."

Sergeant Berenger assisted Kuehn, and Ali followed. Ali was not sure whether Joe was escorting them as enemy or as a friend. They were dressed in enemy uniform, so Berenger understood his immediate concern. Berenger's Australian accent did not diminish his vigilance either way. The trench system wound back and forth down the steep ravine, Kuehn cursing and swearing as he descended.

Sergeant Berenger had never been so glad to hear the clipped New Zealand accent; and their ability to state the obvious through dry understatement.

"Bin in a bit of a war, have you, digger?" said a voice from a troglodyte's hole.

Sergeant Berenger took the bait and responded with a series of well-rehearsed Australian expletives. As it happened, the voice belonged to Lieutenant Colonel Arthur Plugge Commanding Officer of the 3rd Auckland Infantry Regiment. Joe had led Berenger and Ali past Company Headquarters to Battalion Headquarters, which was actually the next hole.

Sergeant Berenger moved the sacking aside, and red-faced went inside. There only just enough room for him to enter. Kuehn was taken for medical treatment and Ali was still under armed guard outside. Berenger was about to offer his sincerest apologies to the New Zealand Commanding Officer when he caught the eye of Commanding Officer's signalman, sniggering away. A mug of something was put into my hand. *Ah, coffee,* Berenger thought. It was tea.

Sergeant Berenger carefully explained the information that he had heard from the Turks, before relating how they were captured on 25 April. He calculated what they did every day from 25 April and related in chronological order it as accurately as possible to Plugge. "But sergeant Berenger, if what you are saying is true, you have missed many days. It is the 18th of May," Plugge enquired. The signalman had called Brigade Headquarters and an intelligence officer soon appeared inside our little cavern.

Sergeant Berenger explained the information that the Turks were planning a massive assault on 19 May. After some extensive examination, especially on how Berenger came to be wearing a German uniform, Berenger restated his account. But for one or two facts that Berenger remembered, he was still short of several days. The intelligence officer looked puzzled. A runner stood outside 3rd Battalion Headquarters.

"Yes," said Plugge, observing two-thirds of an Australian soldier peering through the Hessian sacking dangling in front of his dugout.

"Message from Lieutenant Colonel Price-Weir, Commanding Officer, 10th South Australian Battalion," panted the soldier.

"Go on, then," replied Plugge.

"Lieutenant Colonel respectfully requests the following: bring that bastard Berenger back to battalion."

"Oh!" the ex-school master Plugge exasperated.

There were a number of differences between New Zealand vernacular and Australian vernacular that caused speakers of one dialect confusion when receiving messages from speakers of the other. Price-Weir's meaning in Australian English was that he would be happy to see Berenger: glad that he had made it back alive. Please come back at your soonest convenience to brief me.

Plugge's understanding in New Zealand English of the messenger's meaning was that Price-Weir was unhappy, and Berenger was in a great deal trouble.

Plugge immediately began consoling Berenger.

"Look, you poor old chap. Let's get you out of the uniform."

The signalman produced a New Zealand tunic, trousers and puttees. Berenger did not have the heart to tell Plugge that he would prefer to wear a German uniform rather than a New Zealand one. So, Berenger thanked him for his kind gesture and went outside to change. Ali was gone. Berenger folded up his German uniform and went back inside.

To add insult to injury, Plugge said, "Oh, you look grand. Just like one of us."

Sergeant Berenger merely sighed. He thought it might be opportune to make a request from Plugge.

"Sir, my Commanding Officer has asked for me to return. May I request that I return tomorrow? I still have four men out beyond the New Zealand trenches. They are all in Turkish uniform and I would be able to identify them."

At this moment, a head popped into Plugge's dug out. "Berenger's account confirms our spotter-planes' observations of the past few days concerning the build-up of Turkish troops facing Ari Burnu. The Brigadier has temporarily suspended all but absolutely essential work on the beach. Be prepared to receive reinforcements from the breach within the next 15 minutes." Plugge's little dugout became a hive of activity.

Curtly, he said to Berenger, "OK, yes go," and shooed him away with hand.

Sergeant Berenger made his way to the makeshift armoury. Fortuitously for him, the uniform he was wearing bore the sergeant's stripes of his rank. The soldier at the armoury cleared a weapon and gave it to him without question. Berenger, waiting for ammunition was told, "The ammo will be distributed by the quartermasters in the trench."

So, there were similarities between the New Zealand and Australian army, Berenger thought: damned bureaucracy. Berenger made his way back to the trench from whence he had entered New Zealand lines.

"What are you doing back here? And what are you wearing?" Mackintosh asked. Berenger just looked at him so he could answer his own question as to what it was, he was wearing.

"Alright, you kin sleep over there. It's a bit dangerous though," he pointed to an alcove dug into the trench.

Sergeant Berenger sat down to collect his thoughts. As he leant forward a Turkish round fired from above them struck the wall of the trench, where his head had been.

Bloody Kiwis, he thought, as he drifted off to sleep.

Chapter 16
Rehabilitation

If I should die, think only this of me;
That there's some corner of a foreign field
That is forever England.

The Soldier
Rupert Brooke (1887–1915)

By dawn the trench was full of reinforcements. A new machine-gun post had been sandbagged near where Berenger slept. A 3rd Auckland Infantry Regiment staff sergeant asked Berenger to sign for his ammunition. Thinking about Woolwich, he signed for his rounds. Berenger didn't make life any harder for this soldier than it already was.

It was about 3:30 am, but no Turkish assault. Almost every man was on the parapet waiting for them, but nothing. A second lieutenant was briefing his men that an Australian sergeant had crossed the lines last night and confirmed the reports from the spotter planes: the Turkish assault would be today.

Sergeant Berenger started to doubt whether he had correctly heard or interpreted the information that the Turks would attack. He had not subjected the information to considered critical analysis. Herr General may have been referring to something else. *One doesn't speak in the open about a major attack*, Berenger thought to himself. Even if the language, in which the attack was referred was not the vernacular, the Turkish officers had come out to the road rather than Herr General meeting with them in their command post and there was no reasonable expectation that they would be over-heard by a German-speaking escapee.

Sergeant Berenger started to convince himself that the Turks were not going to attack on the 19th of May. That would be suicide. It was too quiet. He squinted to look between two sandbags. Berenger saw no movement from the Turkish trenches to his front, but then his view was obstructed by the small size of the gap in the sandbags. He observed a white throated kingfisher quietly sitting on a branch of an uprooted arbutus immediately in front of him.

Sergeant Berenger thought about this kingfisher going about its daily business. Had it ever considered its own mortality? Like the insect, it was waiting to eat; the kingfisher's ability to reason was less than human. Berenger wondered about the kingfisher's sentience. The kingfisher feels pain, feels the wind in its wings goes hungry, lives, reproduces and dies.

In their ability to physically suffer, Berenger considered he shared at a least one commonality with the kingfisher. Berenger wondered whether intellect marked out humans for superiority. The kingfisher sat on the knurled branch, shaking its head left and right. Berenger decided that had the kingfisher exhibited any foresight, it should not have remained in No Man's Land.

A strange musing came into Berenger's mind. If the avoidance of suffering both physical and emotional was a raison d'être, why were the Turks to so willing to be slaughtered? The Turks were human too, were they not? Berenger cancelled out the conclusions in his mind several times, in order to rationalise a more satisfactory result but whatever reasoned path he took, he always came to the same answer. Their raison d'être could not be to avoid suffering since their existence was predicated on its continuance.

Sergeant Berenger also had a bad feeling about his interview with the intelligence officer. He was incapable of recalling what happened from about 15 May. Berenger did not tell him about his discussion with the Greek god Pan or that he had seen Cornelia and Juliana in a vision. If he had, Berenger thought the intelligence officer may have had him committed to the sanatorium.

The gentle breeze brought the stench of the dead over the crest of the parapet. An early breakfast in the dark consisted of hardtack and a tin of jam. Someone handed Berenger a mug of something. *Great*, he thought, *coffee*. He dunked his hardtack in it. It was tea: again. He looked up at the parapet. Fifty percent of the reinforcements guarded the defences and 50 per cent were eating or digging.

Despite the chill early morning, Berenger felt himself getting drowsy. He bit his tongue to stay awake. The soldier manning the parapet above him, yawned; raised his head slightly above the sandbags, and he fell back, shot through the head.

"Help that man," Berenger shouted as he climbed into the wounded soldier's newly vacated position.

At that moment, all along the front the machine guns opened up. Yelling and shouting came from the Turkish lines.

"*Allahu Akbar! Allahu Akbar!*"

As the machine guns swept the front, the Turks began to fall. The Company Sergeant Major gave the command for the infantry to fire and an incredible noise reverberated in the trench. Almost the whole front rank of Turks fell to their volley, no more than 50 yards from their position.

The advancing Turks were replaced by another wave and yet another. The bodies piled-up, but then the machine-gun near Berenger jammed. The infantry picked off individual targets; and the machine-gun further to right adjusted its arc of fire.

The Turks were slowly making ground. Hundreds if not thousands had already been killed. Then Berenger saw a huge Turk come thundering down the hill. Berenger recognised his angry face. The angle of the slope assisted his momentum. He was screaming, "*Allahu Akbar!*"

Sergeant Berenger saw him shot. The bullet went into Tolga's stomach but the momentum on his body allowed him to come on. Tolga carried a stick grenade in one hand and his rifle in the other.

Sergeant Berenger could see blood spurting from his wounds and realised Tolga had been shot more than once. Time slowed for Berenger and his focus became more acute. He observed Tolga had also been shot in the face, but Tolga carried on regardless, teeth-bared and screaming with rage. Berenger realised that Tolga too, was trapped in suffering, and had always been trapped in suffering; and his bestial behaviour and baleful existence was a reaction to suffering.

As Tolga threw his grenade, Berenger fired a round into his knee to drop him. Several other rounds from the infantry went into his stomach, chest and face and Tolga fell.

The grenade flew high as if in slow motion. Berenger fired at other targets closing in on him; the grenade went over his head and exploded on top of the parapet behind him.

Sergeant Berenger had no further clear recollection of the 19 May. He was taken to lay with the dead and nearly dead on the beach at Ari Burnu; over-looked by the medics, categorised as less important because he was soon to die: his back a bloodied mess of shrapnel and pulp. His ears were ringing.

Berenger thought he would never forget the exquisite pain of pieces of metal being extracted from his back without anaesthetic at the hospital in Lemnos. He thought he would also never forget the nurses, whose mere presence, kind words and gestures made gravely wounded soldiers fight on to survive. Were it not for the nurses, men with no arms, no legs, disfigured faces and no future would have expired from despair. The doctors and surgeons, however, Berenger regarded as the scientific architects of his agony.

One of the nurses read him poems of Rupert Brooke as he struggled to get comfortable in his dressings. In his mind, the soothing effect of her voice, was a panacea as great any medical procedure administered by the surgeons. Within about a week, Berenger was told that he would be returning to Australia.

"Thank you very much for your service Berenger, but you will be released from the 10th South Australian battalion upon your return to Adelaide," a surgeon advised him perfunctorily.

The surgeon looked at the nurse, who had been reading Berenger poetry. Noting the author from the Times Literary Supplement, he said, "Rupert Brooke, oh, he died on 23 April. Good poet though."

Then he walked away.

Sergeant Berenger lay in his hospital bed, sometimes on his front, sometimes on his side. The pain of his physical wounds gradually began to subside. Between waiting for a nurse to talk to, he made small talk with some of the other patients to try and cheer them up. Some were in a very bad state indeed. There appeared to be no proper treatment for any soldier suffering from psychological trauma; and any solider, who suffered from psychological trauma only, without physical injury, would have instantly been labelled a coward. Young men with terrible facial disfigurements were concerned that their sweethearts would no longer love them when they arrived back in Australia.

When Berenger lay on his side, he could see a large picture of King George V hanging above the door at the entrance to the ward. Berenger often thought about the wounded soldiers, and their uncertain future. None would have had the foresight or the expectation when they were children that they would end their lives crippled and disfigured.

As children many would have had great hopes and expectations. Berenger concluded that the capacity for hope is biological and innate, and that it is environment and culture that diminishes its capacity.

Sergeant Berenger thought about how the ancient Greeks perceived the Fates: Clotho, who spun the thread of life; Lachesis, who measured the length of the thread of life and Atropos, who cut the thread of life with her shares. Laying helpless in their hospital beds, they had become acutely conscious of the precariousness of their lives hanging by a thread. This was an apt metaphor.

But it came to Berenger's mind that their lives had always been precarious. It was their present consciousness of the precariousness, which had altered. Berenger wondered what part consciousness played in existence.

Next to him lay a hapless soldier in a vegetative state. Surely, the dictum "I think, therefore I am" could not apply in the reverse to this poor man, who was presently unable to turn his conscious mind to any thoughts. Surely, the incapacity for human thought does not negate existence. Existence then must be something else.

Sergeant Berenger wondered, what was the effect of consciousness on the dimensions: space and time? He did not think that consciousness was material or made up of atoms. Therefore, consciousness did not occupy space. Consciousness was a concept Berenger believed could exist independent of the body. Therefore, Berenger believed consciousness could not be affected by time. Berenger concluded that consciousness and time were discrete. Consciousness, for Berenger was immutable and it did not diminish because its receptacle, the brain ceased to function, or the body ceased to exist.

Sergeant Berenger looked at King George V hanging in his frame and an idea came upon him. Humans exist within the receptacle of space and time. Outside the receptacle, time and space ceased to exist, but not consciousness.

Perhaps when he experienced the vision of Juliana and Cornelia and then experienced a further vision of them at each stage of their lives, all at the same time, the vision was one not confined by space or time. But the visions were not real, Berenger decided. Culture determined the nature of human visions, but perhaps there was an empirical message behind them.

The concepts of justice and beauty were restricted by the receptacle. The universe was within the same receptacle. Absolute justice and absolute beauty could not exist within the receptacle of the universe if an absolute concept was not subject to the confines of space or time.

Sergeant Berenger wished he could talk to Faber. He wondered whether the search for the origins or the end of the universe was a futile exercise. He decided that the material universe was in itself, like them confined by matter and would constantly be subject to change. The search for existence may better be found in the very small and the very large because Berenger believed they were outside the receptacle.

Existence may be better explained in the probability of an electron being in a particular place at a particular time in an atom; or may be better explained by an objective observer, watching from outside, the universe expanding at an ever-faster rate.

Extrapolating the universe from a point in time to an ultimate end would become meaningless in a dimension, in which time did not exist.

The matter perplexed Berenger deeply. He lay on his side and looked at the picture of the King George V. The frame of his picture proffered many more questions and answers that the subject itself. He was grateful to His Majesty for that.

Going to the toilet became the chore, the manner of which, Berenger objected most intensely. As a severely injured soldier he was barely aware of these daily functions, which the nurses took care of. However, as Berenger became aware of them, he decided it was below his dignity to be assisted in this and moreover it was extremely embarrassing.

The nurses started to complain about Berenger because every time he came back from the toilet, the wounds on his back would bleed through my gown. They euphemistically blamed the strenuousness of his efforts for aggravating them. In any event, they came to a compromise. Berenger would allow one of the nurses to wheel him to the toilet, where he would go in private and then be wheeled back to his bed. Even this caused a few problems where every few minutes or so, a concerned nurse would call out if everything was ok.

Sergeant Berenger refrained from giving her a piece of his mind as he knew some of the other soldiers would continue to be assisted in this manner even when they had returned broken to their loved ones. Berenger's ventures to the toilet became the focus and highlight of his day. The nurses allowed him to bring the odd newspaper to read and once he smuggled his father's copy of 'Crime and Punishment', which to his delight, he finished.

The nurses baulked and confiscated his sketchpad and pencils, which he attempted to smuggle into this cosy repository as they had begun commenting that Berenger was taking too long. By this time, Berenger was fed up with being in hospital and although he hobbled with a severe stoop, he caused a commotion, to which he later apologised profusely.

The whole ward laughed and cheered uproariously, speculating upon what it was that Berenger might be drawing. Inside, he was glad that this episode gave them some cause of mirth and determined that he would compose poetry whilst completing his ablutions. This proved to be quite difficult. Berenger's preliminary efforts in his generally agitated state of mind began as follows:

"Our greatest pleasures may be fulfilled, in the comfort of a cosy repository, without the constraints of time, having a good s s_"

Some days later, after several further mental drafts, in a more contemplative mood this was revised to:

"Nothing great was ever written in a large room."

This would prove prescient, as some years later, the Armistice on 11 November 1918 was signed in the back of a train.

Chapter 17
Awkwardness

"I raised to my lips a spoonful of the tea in which I had soaked a morsel of the cake. No sooner had the warm liquid, and the crumbs with it touched my palate, a shudder ran through my whole body, and I stopped, intent upon the extraordinary changes that were taking place... And at once the vicissitudes of life had become indifferent to me, its disasters innocuous, its brevity illusory – this new sensation having had on me the effect which love has of filling me with a precious essence; or rather this essence was not in me, it was myself."

Marcel Proust
Swann's Way: In Search of Lost Time

It was about a month before a ship was able to take the wounded soldiers home. In that time, Berenger regained the ability to walk, in crippled kind of way. It made him laugh to think about Avraham; the way all his scheming never manifestly improved his financial position. Berenger wondered if he had sold the supplies back to the Ottoman Army.

He thought about Mohammad and Ali. Both were to return to Ibrahim. Ali became part of a prisoner exchange, for Faber and other soldiers captured in the campaign. Second Lieutenant Faber with holes like stigmata in his hands would become a renowned professor of physics.

Although Faber always maintained a belief in God during professor his lectures, he would undermine his own strict rationalism when making a scientific point at odds with Christianity, by inadvertently raising his hands and gesticulating for emphasis. His actions merely attracted gasps from his young physics students, observing his scars.

Tom and the three other escapees travelled in a straight line towards Sulva Bay. Berenger met him in the hospital at Lemnos.

Tom said that they avoided the Turks simply by going around them.

"It was just plain good luck, I s'ppose," he said sheepishly.

Half his face had been blown off on 19 May, so when he smiled, Berenger couldn't tell from his mouth whether his smile was genuine or not. But Berenger guessed from his eyes that it was genuine.

Tom would go back to farming in Queensland. His service was recognised by being awarded a gallantry medal. Tom caught the eye of a pretty girl, who saw this once handsome man, and despite his half face, she fell in love with the other half and his big heart. They were married and soon he had children to concern himself with. The other three men were also decorated with medals. The medals were sent to their families as they were all killed later in the war on the Western Front. Their graves are in France.

Wiremu's spirit is with his ancestors. He is part of the river Waikato in New Zealand. The old people talk of brave Wiremu Tamihana, who was once a Takarangi. The Māori children sit on the banks of the Waikato in the evenings listening to the sounds of the river and watch the sunset. They feel safe when they play in the shallow pools. The children thought the taniwha, who dwells in the deep caverns and bends of the river, could never catch them, with Wiremu's spirit guarding them.

Harry Kuehn went into politics. His incessant complaining during their escape did not abate at parliament. He advocated for the rights of returned servicemen, for medical and psychological treatment of the wounded and for jobs upon repatriation. Berenger has always been hard on people like Kuehn, since they're usually the ones, who get everybody else into these wars. But experience for him was salutary and at least Berenger respected him for that.

Sergeant Berenger felt he spent a lot of time talking to soldiers destined for repatriation in Australia about why his injury was to his back. Each time Berenger finished his now well-rehearsed account, he could not be sure whether the recipient believed a lick of what he was saying. Berenger knew that some of the men destined for New South Wales and Victoria thought he was a damned coward and a liar but there was nothing Berenger could do to change their minds. Berenger began to believe that some of them only wanted a justification of what they thought about South Australian German descendants fighting for the mother country.

Sergeant Berenger tried to look at it from their point of view: young bodies mangled and minds disordered. They were probably in no fit state to make any considered judgements at all. He thought they needed a vent for their frustration. In Berenger's proximity to them, such as the case with de Wet in South Africa, it turned out to be him. So, he didn't begrudge them for it. He felt sorry for them. He knew they were concerned about reuniting with their families.

Sergeant Berenger wondered about Tolga. What created such a beast? Berenger did not think he had been born with such bestial predilections, so Berenger assumed he suffered a sickness of the mind through one or more traumatic experiences during his life. He also considered that a traumatic experience suffered as a child had a deeper impression on the adult than a traumatic experience on a mature adult.

Sergeant Berenger felt his philosophical position had taken a step backwards from whence he had embarked for Gallipoli. His rational stance towards material matters, catalysed by his injury, had been undermined by scepticism and uncertainty. Berenger wondered if his empathetic transformation directed him along the wrong path to ethical answers.

Eventually, the ship docked at Adelaide. Berenger assisted a lot of the injured men off the ship. He didn't mind being the last to disembark, as he thought there was nobody waiting for him and he was a still a little embarrassed with his injury. Berenger walked in a stooped fashion, which would eventually heal but he was self-conscious of it. People would see that the injury was to his back and he was already getting some unusual looks from the families of the other soldiers.

Sergeant Berenger made sure everyone was reunited with their luggage and their loved ones and he shook the hands of a lot of people he did not know. Some of the parents seemed to be embarrassed that their sons were disfigured. Mothers broke into tears and families whisked their loved ones away. Berenger had enough strength to carry his kit bag, which did not contain many possessions, but made his stoop slightly worse.

As he shuffled to where the jetty met the road, where he would have to merge with the pedestrian traffic, a white gloved hand slipped into his free hand.

"Come on, you're going too slow," said a voice Berenger vaguely remembered.

He looked up. It was Juliana. She had grown up. Juliana looked just like her mother. She had her mother's eyes.

"I remembered where you lived," she smiled.

"I wrote to your father. I wrote to you as well, but you did not reply. I've been in Adelaide for almost a month now and I've seen all those places you told me about when we were in Camp K_. I've even seen many wallabies silhouetted on the skyline in the sunset."

"Oh," Berenger said.

"I met your father. Mr Berenger asked me to apologise on his behalf. He couldn't be here to meet you today. He has a court-case in Melbourne and sent me instead," Juliana explained apologetically.

There was an impropriety for a young lady to hold the hand of a man in public, but Berenger enjoyed the feeling of her warm fingers beneath her glove. As he hobbled along, he thought he would exaggerate his stoop just a little so people wouldn't interpret the gesture as too affectionate.

THE END